VOTE

ALSO BY GARY PAULSEN

GARY PAULSEN

VOTE

The Theory, Practice, and Destructive Properties of Politics

A Yearling Book

Text copyright © 2013 by Gary Paulsen
Cover art copyright © 2013 by James Bernardin

All rights reserved. Published in the United States by Yearling, an imprint of Random House Children's Books, a division of Random House, Inc., New York. Originally published in hardcover in the United States by Wendy Lamb Books, an imprint of Random House Children's Books, New York, in 2013.

Yearling and the jumping horse design are registered trademarks of Random House, Inc.

Visit us on the Web! randomhouse.com/kids

Educators and librarians, for a variety of teaching tools, visit us at RHTeachersLibrarians.com

The Library of Congress has cataloged the hardcover edition of this work as follows:
Paulsen, Gary.
Vote : the theory, practice, and destructive properties of politics / Gary Paulsen. — 1st ed.
p. cm.
Summary: Fourteen-year-old Kevin impetuously announces that he will run for student body president, mainly to impress his girlfriend, Tina, but soon gets excited about making a positive difference in his school and community.
ISBN 978-0-385-74228-3 (trade) — ISBN 978-0-375-99053-3 (lib. bdg.) — ISBN 978-0-307-97452-5 (ebook) [1. Politics, Practical—Fiction. 2. Middle schools—Fiction. 3. Schools—Fiction. 4. Interpersonal relations—Fiction. 5. Humorous stories.]
I. Title.
PZ7.P2843Vnt 2013
[Fic]—dc23
2012023059

ISBN 978-0-385-74229-0 (pbk.)

Printed in the United States of America

10 9 8 7 6 5 4 3 2 1

First Yearling Edition 2014

Random House Children's Books supports the First Amendment and celebrates the right to read.

*This book is dedicated
with affection and deep gratitude
to Adrienne Waintraub,
and all the teachers and librarians
she's worked with over the years,
who've done so much for my books
and for young readers.*

foreword

I'm the most gifted leader you'll ever meet.

I should be good; I've had a lot of practice. I'm only fourteen, but I've known for as long as I can remember that some people lead and some people get out of the way. It's a universal rule. A cosmic inevitability.

If you ask me, people who aren't out in front are just looking at someone else's rear end.

My ability to lead is a gift. I must have been born with the innate ability to take control of the situation.

See, people like being around someone who's not afraid to exercise authority.

I've shown my capacity to assume command

1

ever since I first had a name tag stuck on my shirt in kindergarten; I raced to be the line leader every time we went to the drinking fountain or out to the playground for recess. I'm quick to raise my hand to volunteer to head class projects.

I'm the one who took it upon himself to post the emergency exit routes out of our house and put together that disaster survival pack in our crawl space. Upon reflection, a loaf of bread probably wasn't the best item to stash under the family room in case of a terrorist attack or severe-weather warning. But my mother is totally exaggerating when she says she can still smell mold every time she goes downstairs to do the laundry. And I'm pretty sure that forgotten, moldy bread is a valuable survival tool—isn't that how penicillin was invented in the first place?

And I'm the one who showed foresight by bringing the video camera to the baseball play-offs to capture the candid moments of our team in the dugout. I don't care what Dash says, it wasn't my fault that he didn't know he was being filmed and I happened to catch him spitting in Wheels's water bottle because he was mad that Wheels struck out and didn't sacrifice to move Dash to second like he was supposed to.

If you look at it the right way, I'm doing everyone a favor with my initiative.

I'm not bragging or being conceited. I'm just saying what everyone knows deep down.

I don't lie and I don't hustle for money and I don't set up my friends and family to study their reactions.

Not anymore.

I merely recognize my administrative influence, superior people skills and habit of acting definitively in moments of maximum need. I have a knack for being calm, cool and collected.

I used to think like that.

Until my life took a flying leap into the deep end of a nuclear power plant's spent-fuel pool.

1

The True Politician Never Backs Down from a challenge

I was sitting on the front stairs of school Monday morning, waiting for the first bell so I could head to homeroom. I was also watching Tina, who was standing by the flagpole with her friends.

Katrina Maria Zabinski, the World's Most Beautiful, Most Perfect, Best-Smelling Girl. Never in the history of girls has anyone been as . . . radiant as Tina. I looked up pictures of Helen of Troy, Cleopatra, Mata Hari and Nefertiti and, even though they're supposed to be world-class babes, they've got nothing on Tina. In fact, I thought they were kind of horrible-looking, but when you've seen perfection up close and in person, everything else seems dismal in comparison. Especially if all you have to go by is ancient artwork that usually makes them look super crabby.

I was now Tina's official boyfriend. I no longer had to worry about how to *get* her. Now I was panicked about how to *keep* her.

We'd had a great time at my neighbor Betsy's grandparents' fiftieth-anniversary party a week ago. It had been everything I'd ever dreamed of—me and Tina talking and laughing and eating chunks of banana dipped in the chocolate fountain. The perfect first date.

I freaked out after the party, though, and reverted to form last week at school.

Which meant that I fell over my own feet every time I saw her and, for conversation, made sounds like the dinosaurs probably did the nanosecond they saw the giant meteorite hurtling toward them. She didn't seem to mind, she'd smile and wave as I hurried away from her, so I didn't make a bad situation worse. But I couldn't count on her tolerance forever. If you want a girl like that to stay your girlfriend, you've got to raise your game.

I had to find a way to impress her. Fast.

"Hey." My best buddy, JonPaul, appeared as if

out of thin air. That's the thing: when Tina's around, I don't notice anything else. A volcano could erupt next to me and I wouldn't flinch. Unless, of course, the molten lava threatened Tina's safety, in which case I like to think I'd swoop in to save her. Kevin Spencer: middle school superhero.

"Hey." I watched JonPaul pull Baggies of edamame and slivered almonds and dried figs out of his messenger bag. He's a health nut and a jock and he eats the ugliest food on the planet. This was his post-breakfast, pre-midmorning-snack snack. He's obsessed with fueling his body for optimum performance on the field. On the court. In the ring. Whatever. I can never keep track of what sport he's playing.

"What are you doing sitting on the steps all by yourself?" He slurped from a bottle of pulverized-seaweed juice. I shuddered at the scummy green mustache it left behind.

"Watching Tina."

"Why?"

"She's beautiful."

"If you say so." JonPaul had a girlfriend of his own, Sam, and wasn't the kind of shady boyfriend who'd notice other girls. Even if they were shockingly gorgeous. "Why are you just watching her? Thought you two were official."

"We are. Kind of. Sort of. I guess." I was about to explain my dilemma when I noticed Cash Devine working his way through the crowd, handing out buttons, flashing his big phony smile and shaking hands. He was wearing a sandwich board—VOTE 4 CA$H.

"What's he doing?" Cash is my mortal enemy. He doesn't realize I can't stand him, but I've loathed Cash from the moment I saw him two weeks ago, when he transferred to our school and latched on to Tina. Cash looks exactly like the kind of guy who should be dating a girl who looks like Tina. Therefore, I spend a great deal of time thinking about how he annoys me.

"Running for student-body president."

"Don't we already have one?"

"Not anymore. Danny Donnerson moved."

"What's with all this moving all of a sudden? Don't today's parents care about providing stability for their kids—and their kids' classmates— anymore?"

"Dunno." JonPaul stays pretty detached when I rant and rave. He's very calming that way.

Just then Cash headed for the group of girls standing near the flagpole.

He headed toward Tina.

The same primal instinct that prompted the cavemen to wave spears in the air when the woolly mammoth came too close kicked in and I was on my feet, barreling toward my competition.

I arrived at Tina's circle of friends just as Cash was reaching out to hand her a button; I slid between them at the last second. He jerked his hand back and jabbed himself in the leg with the pin.

"Oh, hey, Cash, you okay there? Gotta be careful," I said, hoping Tina would appreciate the concern in my voice and not realize how insincere I was.

"Uh, yeah, I'm good. First blood of the campaign season," he guffawed, sounding exactly like the guy on the local-access cable channel who's way too excited about selling used cars. "Can't win an election without a little wear and tear." He looked over my shoulder and winked at the girls.

I heard a collective sigh and turned to face Tina and her friends. JonPaul had Tina holding one of his gluten-free rice cakes while he drizzled organic honey on it, so she, thank the gods of love, wasn't one of the sighers. Connie Shaw and Katie Knowles, my sorta friends, were two of the girls oohing and aahing over Cash. I felt a stab of jealousy even though I'm with Tina and I don't like Katie and Connie that way.

"Cash is going to run for student-body president," Katie told me, a soft look on her face as she gazed at Cash. A flyer she'd been holding fluttered to the ground. I stooped to pick it up.

CA$H 4 PRE$IDENT.

That's it? Three measly words. And one was a misused number! I flipped over the so-called campaign literature to see if I was missing the meaty message. We'd just finished a section in social studies on the American political process, so I knew that a voter should expect dazzling rhetoric and impressive verbiage.

Nope. Nothing. The other side of the paper was blank. I shook my head: I've written more engrossing and persuasive text messages. The slogan, if that's what you call it, was underneath a huge head shot of Cash, winking and flashing a combination double thumbs-up/finger pistols. Totally cheesy and lame.

Too bad the girls didn't think so. They were staring at him. Either they'd used a real heavy hand with the makeup that morning or they were coming down with fevers, because they were all rosy-cheeked.

Ick.

I peeked at Tina. JonPaul, good man, had accidentally dribbled honey on her, so she was paying more attention to her sticky sleeve than to Cash's cry for attention. He's so obvious.

"I'm running too." I hoped I didn't look as surprised as I felt to hear my own voice blurt that out. I jammed a hand behind my back to cross my fingers, hoping that I looked casual, almost bored, like I made announcements like this all the time.

I hadn't woken up that morning planning to run for student-body president, but it's undemocratic to have a candidate run unopposed. This is how third world countries begin to languish under oppressive regimes. Besides, I couldn't let Cash steal the spotlight.

"You are?" JonPaul choked on a rice cake.

"*You* are?" Katie gave me a cool once-over.

"You *are*?" Connie clapped her hands.

The other girls were all staring at Cash as if he were the embodiment of every member of every boy band on the planet.

Double ick. But their mindless adoration of his surface perfection stiffened my resolve.

"Yes." I lifted my chin, wishing a sudden gust of wind would ruffle my hair and make me look rugged. Rugged and determined and a little like a male model.

Tina, who was patting JonPaul's back because he was still yakking up rice cake, smiled at me, and as my heart skipped a beat, I knew I had the perfect opportunity to dazzle her. Girls like Tina were born to date student-body presidents. "I didn't get a chance to, uh, mention, my, um, intentions before, but, yeah, I—"

"I'll help you," Connie blurted out. She's very politically minded, and ever since we'd worked together on a debate in front of the city council a few weeks back, she'd been forwarding me articles about, um, whatever it was we'd argued in favor of. Or against. It was really boring, and I only paid attention to the details long enough to fake my way through the meeting. I'm good like that: I know exactly how long I need to retain information before I can purge it in favor of something new. I have a mind like a constantly upgrading computer operating system.

"Glad I can count on you," I told Connie. Before I could turn to Tina and ask for her support, or at least her vote, if not yet her hand in marriage, Katie spoke up.

"Cash," she said in a tone that made my stomach clench up, "I'd like to offer my services to *your* campaign." I bet that Katie's sudden interest probably had less to do with Cash's qualities and more to do with his perfect smile. And the fact she doesn't trust me as far as she can throw me. We've had a few . . . misunderstandings in the past that have made me one of her least favorite people.

Volunteering to work on Cash's campaign gave Katie the chance to spend more time with him and get under my skin. Good one, Katie, I thought; you're so devious and forward-thinking, you could almost be me.

She caught my eye and we nodded, like two

13

gunfighters in the Old West before they turned and counted off paces. She knew and I knew: Cash and I might be running against each other, but Katie and I were the ones who would be fighting it out.

Game on.

2

The True Politician
Seizes the Day

I don't dislike Katie, and we've had a few nice moments where we've clicked as friends, but we mostly seem to get on each other's nerves. The combined force of our personalities repels us from one another. They say nature abhors a vacuum, but it doesn't like two take-charge personalities in the same vicinity either.

I keep trying to get along with Katie, but it never seems to work out. And I could tell from the looks we gave each other that we weren't about to start getting chummy now. But I wasn't going to let something personal distract me. I was in this race to win. I'd harness our tension as inspiration; her . . . antipathy toward me would motivate me to do my best. Every politician needs a worthy opponent, and from what I'd seen of Cash, he wouldn't give me the run for my money that I knew Katie would. This way, I'd impress Tina, put dopey Cash in his place *and* become a seasoned veteran of a hard-fought political war by defeating Katie's candidate. Which was perfect, because everyone knows that good things come in threes.

The second after Katie and I silently acknowledged the battle lines, the bell rang. We sprinted toward the building, weaving between slow-moving students and leaping the front steps in single bounds, neck and neck as we crossed the foyer. I gained a few feet on her when Mrs. Nickerson, the home ec teacher, stopped to sip from her cup of coffee. Katie dodged to the left and missed knocking Mrs. Nickerson over, but the maneuver cost her valuable seconds and I raced down the hall ahead of her.

Katie is surprisingly speedy for such a bookish girl, and she gained on me, so we burst through Mr. Crosby's door at the same time, skidding to a stop in front of his desk.

He's our social studies teacher and the faculty

advisor to the student government. He had the forms we needed to fill out to register as presidential candidates. If she hadn't been my opposition, I'd have been impressed by the way great minds think alike and how Katie and I had known that we had to get to Mr. Crosby to make these campaigns official.

"Well, this doesn't look good," he said, glancing up from his newspaper. "Whatever prompted the two of you to come flying into my room like small winged creatures from Hades can't possibly be in the best interest of this school. Or me."

"Heh heh heh." Katie and I gave the exact same forced laugh and then glared at each other. "I'm running for president," we both said. Mr. Crosby raised his eyebrows. So did I.

"I mean, Cash is running for president. It's Cash, not me. Cash," Katie corrected herself, looking flustered. Katie always has her facts straight, and I was fascinated to see her deteriorate in front of my very eyes. "Cash and Kevin are running. Against each other. And I'm his campaign manager. I'm Cash's. Cash's campaign manager, that is, not his, um . . . " Katie was about to implode next to me.

She was saved when Cash and Connie straggled

into Mr. Crosby's room. Cash's sandwich board was hanging from one shoulder; the string had broken in the crowded hall. Passing between classes can be brutal, especially when you're wearing poster board. Note to self: extend passing time. That'll be my first campaign promise. Man, five minutes into this campaign and already I'm coming up with genius ideas. I'm a natural. I'm just sorry I wasn't of service to the citizens of this school sooner. They need me.

"What's going on here?" Mr. Crosby was studying us skeptically. I did a double take when I saw that Connie was clutching Cash's hand; he must have grabbed her to follow us when Katie and I took off. She didn't look unhappy to be holding on to him, nor did she look like she was going to let go. He had to pry her fingers off before he could turn on the charm for Mr. Crosby.

"We haven't met because I have Mrs. Skraw for social studies." Cash leaned across the desk and pumped Mr. Crosby's hand in a hearty handshake. "I'm Cash Devine, your next president."

Connie reached for Cash's hand again. "Kevin has decided to run too."

"Against Cash." Katie jerked him away from

Connie and took a firm hold of his hand herself. "And he has—had—a sandwich board announcing his candidacy. He came prepared to win." Katie let go of Cash's hand, but only so she could tie the frayed ends of the string together and readjust the sign on his shoulders, before gently pushing him behind her so she and I were shoulder to shoulder in front of Mr. Crosby and Cash was out of reach of Connie.

I looked back at Cash and noted that the sandwich board was still crooked and that his dollar sign had fallen off. VOTE 4 CA H. *Cah* is the sound a cat makes when it throws up, I thought. Fitting, since Cash is a hairball of a candidate. I read once that your thoughts can be seen on your face, so I put on a cheerful expression before I turned to Mr. Crosby.

"Oh, hey, instead of, you know, with all the disruption and distraction and, um, dissension of the whole election process"—I looked meaningfully at Katie—"what do you say you just pick a president, Mr. Crosby?" Being appointed would be even better than running. Less worry and effort, more prestige. Besides, he doesn't know Cash from a hole in the wall and he loves me. Or likes me. Or at least recognizes me from class. I edged closer to the desk and tried to look presidential.

"Oh no. Don't make the mistake of thinking you can rope me into this mess, Kev." Mr. Crosby and I have a history of misunderstandings, so I guess I can't blame him for not taking me up on my suggestion. "I don't even know if this school has an official policy for a student government vacancy, but, by the power vested in me by . . . by virtue of being faculty advisor because no one else volunteered, I'm creating one now: 'In the event that the president cannot complete his or her term, an election will be called within one week's time to elect a replacement.'"

Katie and I smirked at each other. Cash checked his hair in the reflection of a shiny letter opener he picked up off Mr. Crosby's desk, and Connie snapped a picture of me with her phone. At least, I think it was of me. She might have been aiming at Cash.

"The election will be Friday during lunch." Mr. Crosby started edging out of the room. "I'll go make the announcement during, um, morning announcements. Good luck, thank you for your service to your school and keep it clean."

I was pretty offended that he directed the last warning to me alone and kind of bummed that he didn't spot my leadership potential and just name me president. But then I decided to look on the bright side—because the chief characteristics of a great politician are, um, optimism and . . . being a natural-born campaigner. That's me.

I was ready. Not to mention happy and relieved that we didn't have to fill out any forms after all. Paperwork is not my thing.

Great things happen to great people. I'm convinced of that, whaddayacallit, truism, yeah, something that's true. I mean, just look at me: one minute I'm just sitting there, trying to think of a way to show I'm worthy of being Tina's boyfriend, and then, bang, an entire presidential election is pretty much handed to me. The second homeroom bell hasn't even rung yet and already I've taken action that not only will change the course of my life, but also is likely to alter the history of this entire school.

Actually, when you think about it, I hadn't even had to take action; action had been thrust upon me. Fate called. Or was it duty? Which one calls? Well, whatever was taken or thrust or whoever called:

Kev's life was falling into place. I would run the greatest campaign this school had ever seen, I'd win the vote—and get the girl—and all would be right with the world.

Man, it is good to be me sometimes, it really is.

3

The True Politician Plays to His Strengths

I practically floated out of Mr. Crosby's office, headed toward homeroom. I was psyched. This was the most foolproof plan ever for impressing Tina.

While it's true that my latest run of good ideas and awesome plans hadn't been a hundred percent successful, I'm not the kind of guy who lets a few failures get him down. That's another key component of a great political candidate: undauntability. If that isn't a word, I'm going to pass a law and make it one, because that's what this country in general, and this school in particular, needs more of: undauntability. It's a word that will look great on a bumper sticker.

A lot had gone wrong for me in the past. But this time, I thought, will be different. Because I'm not just *thinking like* a politician, I'm actually *becoming* one. I'm not just *acting like* my role model, I *am* the role model. That is going to make all the difference. See, in the past, I'd taken lessons learned from other areas and tried to apply them to the situation I was facing. *That* had been my downfall. It had been the overall conception, not my specific implementation, that had been faulty. But the disasters, or rather, growth opportunities of my recent past were behind me. I was unstoppable.

I found my way out of homeroom and to my first-period class, where I took notes the entire time. Not on the lecture—they were discussing *The Wizard of Oz*, a novel that creeped me out as much as the movie version. Put the dog on a leash, Dorothy! I could handle the flying monkeys and even the house falling on the witch, but I couldn't stop obsessing about Toto running around loose. I'm a little obsessive or else a huge advocate of pet safety to worry like that. Animal lover, I decided, jotting that down in my notebook. Voters don't put their trust in candidates who demonstrate obsessive streaks, but everyone loves—and is happy to vote for—someone who loves pets.

I'm also a people person. I wrote to myself, "Kev likes animals AND people." Another quality that was going to come in handy. I was just filled to the brim with characteristics that made me electable. All that was left was to let the student body know.

I didn't have any time to waste, since I was dealing with a warp-speed, five-day campaign season. First: whip through the school day gathering support. Which might consist of bellowing in the halls to each and every person I knew by name, "I'm running for student-body president! Vote for me on Friday!"

Even though I know pretty much everyone in school because I'm an eighth grader and, let's face it, lovable, there had to be a more efficient way of making myself known than hollering at every student. I needed to win over entire clumps of voters. What do they call them on TV during the presidential elections? Caucuses? Constituency? Cohort? Cormorants? Some C-word.

Note to self: dig out the thesaurus. No one likes to watch someone fumble for the, whatchamacallit, right words. Also: carry note cards. Everyone always looks smarter referring to note cards. Even if they're blank. I can't prove it, but I'm sure teachers grade higher when they see that you've summarized your presentation on note cards; it shows you've done the work ahead of time. And, besides, a teleprompter would be, um, pretentious. And out of my budget, which is zero. And hard to carry through the hallway, while ruining the element of spontaneity. A guy like me has to take advantage of spur-of-the-moment opportunities to make strong impressions.

Oh, good, my first dilemma and I was handling it masterfully. Granted, I was just sitting in class taking notes. But the important thing was that I was working the problem, the problem wasn't working me, and it was good experience for later. Political people are judged by how they handle a crisis. By that standard, I'm a golden child.

Who should I speak with first? I tapped my pencil against my notebook and concentrated. What's the first interest group to approach? Teachers don't vote. A real shame, considering how I've endeared myself to the faculty and staff, the recent bout with skipping classes and lying to everyone notwithstanding. But, hey, who hasn't had a rough patch? It's what makes the common man identify with a public figure. Smart move, Kev—in hindsight, a brilliant strategy. Even my goofs are helpful to me if I regard them in the proper perspective.

I thought back to how the girls had feasted on Cash this morning. He'd locked down the female vote just because he was good-looking. And I couldn't afford to lose half of the eighth grade right off the bat. Unless I got the younger girls on my side. Cash's brand of physical perfection was probably intimidating to unworldly sixth- and seventh-grade girls. I'd play up my boy-next-door quality and win their trust. Given that I'd lived in this town my whole life and Cash had just invaded—I mean moved here—two weeks ago, I could consider "protective older brother to the younger girls" my turf.

Enter Milania Zeman, captain of the girls' junior varsity basketball team, my entrée to the sixth- and seventh-grade female population.

I'd always considered Milania Zeman to be a shrill-voiced demon-brat, the kind of girl who's likely to wind up on a reality television show, pulling her best friend's hair and throwing food at her grandmother during a family gathering. But the younger girls in this school worship her because

27

she almost single-handedly led the squad to state last year. This school is known for dismal sports teams (sorry, JonPaul, but it's a fact), so her success was a big deal. She was scary, but her influence was impressive.

Major bummer, though: I'd recently disagreed with her over who had dibs on the gym for practice. Excuse me, but the basketball team *can* run laps in the hallway, whereas the wrestling squad, of which I was a member briefly until another recent misunderstanding, *has* to use the gym because that's where the mats are located. And no one ever died waiting twenty minutes for someone else to get done using the gym. Enough said.

Except to Milania, who argued with me loudly enough for the wrestling coach to ask, in the interest of the team, for me to resign to make peace with Milania, because the girls' JV basketball team were defending state champions, and upsetting their practice time would lead directly to them losing state this year, which would then cause the Earth to slip off its axis and slide out of its rotation and crash into the sun. Or something.

To tell the whole truth, Milania had done me a

solid, since I wasn't unhappy to hang up my singlet and retire with a 0–0 record. "Undefeated athlete," I jotted in my notes. The public loves successful jocks.

Milania and I had gotten off on the wrong foot, but that was nothing we couldn't repair with a good sit-down over lunch today. Face to face, we'd find common ground and become pals, after which she'd swing the vote of the sixth- and seventh-grade girls in my favor.

I'd have the underclass girls in my back pocket by sixth period today. Not bad, Kev, not bad at all.

As soon as I got to the lunchroom, before I could even look for Milania, a hand grabbed my T-shirt from behind and yanked me nearly off my feet, dragging me into a corner next to the milk cooler.

"I hear that pretty boy Cash Devine is running for president," Milania snarled as I checked to see if she'd crushed my windpipe when she'd heaved me out of the milk line.

"Uh, yeah, I heard that too," I said cautiously, smoothing my shirt back in place.

"I need you to run against him. And win."

Interesting. "Why?"

"Donnerson and I had an agreement. Now he's gone. I need someone in the student government who can see reason."

"Agreement?"

"Look, a school our size doesn't have a JV basketball team going to state championships without help from friends in high places. Understand?"

"Not even a little bit."

"Danny always made sure to arrange pep rallies for us on the days of our big games."

"And?"

"Pep is *everything*. Support from the fans is the sixth player on the court."

"I had no idea you felt so strongly about school spirit."

"It's what I live for. I used to be a really awful person before I found sports and was able to channel my aggression into a positive outlet."

You mean there was a *worse* version of you? Yikes.

Milania was still talking: "If I didn't have basketball, I can't even imagine how I'd wind up."

I could, but I didn't share my mental image of her on that reality TV show.

"Why me? Why don't you run against him if you know what you want from student government?"

"I admire you. A little." She narrowed her eyes as she studied me. A chill ran down my spine as I hoped that middle school basketball really was going to be enough to keep her on the right path and away from becoming a violent, fame-seeking she-devil; sports heroes have the possibility of college scholarships, whereas angry mini-dictators face limited occupational opportunities. She continued, "You stood up to me, and that's more than anyone else did."

That's because people are frightened of you, I said silently, hoping she couldn't read my thoughts on my face. Note to self: practice blank faces in the mirror. And trustworthy smiles. And serious concern.

"Oh, well, I guess, I mean . . ."

"And I can make sure you'll get elected. I'll make sure you have the support you need to beat Cash. People listen to me."

They tremble in fear, but sure, I can see why you'd put it differently. I nodded.

"So, what are you going to do?" Milania locked

her eyes on me. I am so glad I'm not a girl and I don't play basketball, because that is not a look I'd want to see aimed in my direction with nothing more than a ref with a whistle to protect me.

"The only thing I can: run against him. But only because I see your need." I tried to sound a little reluctant so she'd feel like she had talked me into this. It's always good for people to think they owe you favors. I think that's what they call political currency. Man, I am so glad Dad and I just watched that movie about the newspaper reporters who went after the president.

"Thanks. Remember: pep rallies the day of every game. It's essential."

Yeah, yeah, I thought, or else the Earth will collide with the sun. I smiled and nodded, feeling powerful. Ask and it shall be done.

I'd already struck my first political deal and I hadn't even cracked open my lunch bag.

I. Am. Awesome.

4

The True Politician Carefully Builds a Strong Support Team

I'd planned to ask if I could borrow Aunt Buzz's conference room for my campaign headquarters—she runs her own interior design business—so I told JonPaul and Connie to meet me there after school. I was all set to blast straight over to talk to Buzz when I got a text from Mom: "GETHOMENOW." Actually I received two texts; the first read "GETHOMENOW" and the second was 160 exclamation points.

What the . . . ?

Oh. Right. Markie.

Markie's my four-year-old neighbor, and I babysit him once a week. The relationship started because I needed the money. Then it morphed into an I'm-a-good-influence-on-him-because-his-folks-are-splitting-up situation. Soon our arrangement became a Markie's-good-for-me-because-he's-surprisingly-wise-for-a-preschooler dealeo.

He's staying at our house for a few days because his parents have gotten back together and are going on a second honeymoon. I feel partly responsible for saving their marriage; but that's another story.

The point is: Markie's parents had dropped him at our house that morning on their way out of town. Mom and Dad were each taking some time off work to watch Markie during the day with the understanding that as soon as I got home from school, they didn't want to know we had a Markie under our roof. Fair enough.

Mom might have gotten a smidge tired of Markie by now. I love him, but a little goes a long way and Mom hasn't got my knack with children. Plus, she's old. You have to be young and fresh and on your toes to cope with Markie.

So I power walked home. Not only was I hurrying home to assume my responsibilities (another excellent character asset in anyone aspiring to hold public office), but I was getting in shape and building stamina. The voting public likes healthy candidates who are in tip-top physical shape.

"Dutchdeefuddy." Markie was waiting for me on our front stoop. He greeted me with his special name for me; it means best, most favorite buddy in the world forever. I waved at him, bent over, put my hands on my knees and tried to catch my breath. As I waited for the stitch in my side to subside, I congratulated myself on my foresight in holding my first workout so privately. Man, those bananas dipped in melted chocolate chips I'm always eating haven't done me any favors.

"Hey, Markie," I said when I could talk and breathe at the same time. "What are you doing on the front stoop?" I dropped down next to him.

Markie handed me a bottle of water from his backpack, which looks like a baby panda, and I chugged half the bottle.

"After we read eighteen picture books and made a fort out of pillows—do you know there are twenty-two pillows in your house and they're all in the family room right now and only four are wet?— and played hide-and-seek with the cat—see my scratch?—and ate worm cookies—that's what I call the cookies with the chopped-up figs but it made your mom gag a little—and I still didn't want to take a nap because I'm four and not a baby anymore, she said I should sit outside and think quiet thoughts until you got home and we both went far away for a long time. Do you want some more water?"

"Yeah, do you have another bottle in that backpack bear?"

"No, but there's a puddle in the backyard."

"Did I just drink water from the ground?"

"No." But he was nodding yes.

Gross. But I had bigger things to think about than water. I popped a mint, hoping it would freshen my breath and kill any yard bacteria I'd just picked up. "C'mon, Markie, we're going to Auntie Buzz's office."

"I love Auntie Buzz." Markie smiled and slipped his hand in mine as we headed toward Buzz's office. Of course Markie was crazy about Buzz; they're both a little on the loony side. And I say that with love. Markie and Auntie Buzz are two of my favorite people. But they're both a few crayons short of a full box.

I sent Mom a text on the way, letting her know the house was a Markie-free zone for a few hours.

We stopped by the bakery across the street from Buzz's office. Sustenance. We both ordered a custard-filled doughnut, but then I remembered that Markie's only four and needs to eat a healthy and well-balanced diet, so I changed his order to a mini–apple pie. Fruit is the cornerstone of any four-year-old's snack time.

"It's tiny," Markie said. "It's like I'm a giant and this is a regular-sized pie. Can we buy some magic beans so I can grow a beanstalk in the backyard?"

"Maybe later. Here, hold my doughnut while I put more sugar in the triple espresso for Auntie Buzz. Oh—hey, Goob, didn't see you."

Goober is JonPaul's cousin and he'd gotten a job at the bakery because of me a few weeks back. I'd turned the owner on to a lucrative side business selling pastries at the local college's dorms during study time. Goober had been hired to make the deliveries.

"Kevinnnnnn." He air high-fived me since I had my hands full of espresso and Markie, who'd moved closer and grabbed my hand when he saw Goober. I can't blame him. Goober had recently texted me to tell me he'd started growing dreadlocks. He's pale and freckled, with bright red hair, and I don't think he had the hang of how to start new dreads. At least, I hoped not. He looked . . . clumpy. I peered closer and saw that he'd gathered sections of his hair in multicolored scrunchies and then twisted them around like some really horrible version of bed head. Dude, I thought, scrunchies are so out. Even little girls don't wear scrunchies anymore. And Rastas with real dreads have never worn elasticized tubes of patterned fabric.

"I like your hair," Markie whispered from behind my legs. "Did you get in trouble for doing that?"

"Little dude." Goober grinned down at Markie and then looked back at me. "You didn't tell me you had a kid! This. Is. Blowing. My. Mind. Kev has his own kid."

"Uh, Goob? I'm fourteen. He's not mine. He's just a friend."

"Sure, 'just a friend.'" He did air quotes with his fingers and wrinkled his face at me. "No worries. I don't judge. Guy in my poli-sci class, he brings a 'friend' in a baby carrier on his back to class. It's all good. Oh, wow"—he noticed Markie's backpack—"I'll trade you my wallet chain for that panda."

"Deal." I watched them hook Goober's chain to a belt loop on Markie's cargo pants and wrap it around his waist to take up the slack—Goober is very tall and Markie is, well, four. Goober couldn't fit his arms through the panda straps, so he held the backpack like a baby.

"Okay," I told them, heading for the door, "now that the accessories exchange is complete: this espresso is burning a hole in my hand. Over to Buzz's office."

"Who has a crazy name like Buzz?" Goober petted the panda.

"Well, gee, *Goober*, that *is* a crazy name, isn't it?" He nodded and rolled his eyes, totally missing my point. I sighed and explained, "It's my aunt's nickname because she drinks too much coffee. Her office is across the street, and JonPaul and Connie are meeting me there to discuss helping me run for student-body president."

"Can I come with? I just stopped by to pick up my check. Be nice to see JP."

"Yeah, sure, take Markie's hand while we cross the street." I probably should have told Markie to take Goober's hand; Markie's got more common sense and always remembers to look both ways.

This'll be fun, I thought: Markie, Goober and Buzz in the same room. But then I realized that no politician has ever gotten to choose their public. They play the hand that's dealt them, citizen-wise, and so would I. Speaking in front of my family and friends would be good experience, since none of them, obviously, could vote for me, but I could still practice my speeches on them and use them as a focus group for, uh, whatever focus groups are used for. Connie would know. I'd leave details like that to her and concentrate on the fun things like affecting public policy and being adored.

We ran across the street and burst into Buzz's office. I handed her the coffee and, hot as it was, she tossed it back in three gulps. She didn't take a breath. Her esophagus is either made of cast iron or lined with scar tissue.

I noticed Goober eying her appreciatively. Goober has a thing for my mother, I found *that* out a couple weeks ago, and Mom and Auntie Buzz share a strong family resemblance.

"Betsy," I hissed, reminding him of his girl-friend when he shifted the panda to his left hand and leaned forward to introduce himself to Buzz. He slapped his forehead and took a step back. I can't blame him for forgetting; the idea of someone like Goober having a girlfriend, especially one as . . . literate and clinically sane as Betsy, is hard to wrap your mind around. He smiled at Buzz, though, and nudged me, nodding. I shook my head at him: no hitting on my relatives.

"Ooh, blocks!" Markie and his new wallet chain jangled across the room. Buzz has a worktable full of wooden blocks in her reception area. She uses them for, um, spacial relativity or, uh, something, when she starts putting together rooms. I only know that much because Sarah and Daniel and I bought them for her for Christmas one year. Goober loped over to the block table and started divvying up the arches and columns between him and Markie. Hours of fun. That'd keep them busy while I negotiated space with Buzz and started the meeting when JonPaul and Connie arrived. I felt a sudden kinship with working parents, who have to occupy their kids while they try to get things done.

Look at that: one day into the campaign and already I was developing empathy with people I didn't have anything in common with. So many awesome examples of my innate political ability had been wasted in this single day because no one had been there to witness them. Dang.

"You won't be holding illegal gambling on my property again, will you?" Buzz narrowed her eyes and studied me. I'd hosted a small card game in her office the last time I'd asked to sublease from her.

"Of course not. I don't gamble anymore. Or lie. Or play matchmaker. I'm running for office."

"Uh-huh. You say that like it's a step up from your past behavior."

"See, that's the problem: today's citizen is skeptical of the political process. Too much empty dialogue, too many broken promises. I aim to change all that."

"Sure you do. Well, okay, if you want to run for president, be my guest. But if I see so much as one playing card on my premises, I'm going to smack your behind so hard your grandchildren's grandchildren will be born with stinging buttocks." She filled her cup with coffee, huffed back to her office and slammed the door.

"I'll just go see if I can help her," Goober said, practically leaping across the office and rat-a-tat-tatting on her door. Markie followed him, an armful of building blocks clutched to his chest.

Whew! It's official: we have office space for the

campaign. Now I just needed some staff. I turned and saw JonPaul, Connie and JonPaul's girlfriend, Sam, opening the door.

Things were about to start getting good. I now had people on-site who would bear witness to my greatness and help me make the world a better place, one middle school at a time.

I felt the same sudden surge of energy and optimism that Thomas Jefferson must have felt when he signed the Louisiana Purchase papers with France. Or was he the one who bought Florida from Spain? Well, it must have totally rocked for him back then, just like it did for me right now.

5

The True Politician
IS Not Afraid to Fly Solo

Before I could open my mouth, JonPaul gave a huge yawn, Sam sniffled and wiped tears from her cheeks, and Connie, who had her nose buried in a textbook, walked into a coffee table.

"Great, glad you're all here. You too, Sam, even though you don't go to our school. Why are you crying?"

"MyhamsterHumphreydied." Even in grief, Sam talks superfast. I was surprised she hadn't owned a chipmunk, because she sounds like one sometimes.

Bummer about the little guy kicking the bucket. News of the recent death of a loved one is a real downer in terms of launching the campaign season with a bang. So I did what all good politicians do when faced with a potentially awkward situation: I ignored it and moved on. With purpose and power, because then it's not rude, it's just presidential.

"Okay! As every student of the political arena knows, there are five crucial stages we must address as we become a well-oiled machine dispensing political clout and civic-minded, uh, greatness."

"Oh, wait: I know this one." JonPaul raised his hand like he was in class. "The five stages of sleep. Did I tell you that I just figured out that my rest is neither restorative nor recuperative like the fancy mattress advertisement says it should be?"

"Uh, no, you didn't mention that."

"Yeah, well, it's true. My theta waves and sleep spindles, you know, light sleep, are in good shape."

"We're all grateful to hear that."

As usual, JonPaul missed my sarcasm. "I know, right? But my delta waves and REM, that's where I'm all messed up. Oh, wait, that's only four. See, I'm so tired I'm losing memory function."

"And this is important because . . . ?" As much as I know I shouldn't encourage JonPaul to obsess about issues surrounding his health, sometimes I can't help egging him on. He's a germaphobe, a gym rat and a health nut, and it's pretty good humor listening to him discuss the dangers of microorganisms, his fitness routine and what he puts in his body and how it later comes out. The fixation on rest was new, though.

"There is no way I can repair the damage to and encourage the growth of healthy cells if I'm not resting adequately. I'm aging faster than I should. Do you know what that's going to do to my athletic career if I'm already a fourteen-year-old in a twenty-two-year-old body?"

"Sounds rough, buddy, and I feel for you, but the five stages of sleep are not what we're discussing. Does anyone else have a guess?" I could have just told them, but real leaders encourage those around them to think for themselves. We lead people to discover great ideas on their own, we don't just hand them out for free.

"It'sthefivestagesofgrief," Sam answered, sniffling. "Denial, anger, bargaining, depression and acceptance."

"Uh, no. But, again, sorry you're having such a rough time, Sam. It must be, um, painful to have lost your hamster."

"Hamsters are hindgut fermenters," Markie

said. He'd deserted Buzz and Goober and was building a castle on the floor next to me, his panda backpack once again clinging to his shoulders.

"How do you know that and what does that even mean?" Leave it to Markie to have the best vocabulary in the room.

"Your mom and I read it in a book this morning. Hamsters eat their own poopies."

"They do not."

"Actually, they do." Connie looked up from her studying. "Hamsters ingest their feces in order to digest their food a second time, a practice known as coprophagy."

"Why would anyone do that, even a hamster?"

"To obtain the proper nutrients from its food."

"That is grosser than drinking mud-puddle water like I did earlier and I don't want to talk about this anymore. Time to get back on the beam. Does *anyone* know what five things I'm trying to get you to name?"

"Is it the five stages of mitosis?" Connie murmured, her nose buried in her notebook. "Because I have a test on cell division tomorrow, and it would be super helpful if we could review that chapter together." She absentmindedly handed Sam another tissue and turned a page.

"No, group development. I've been reading up on this and—you're going to love this—the key elements are forming, storming, norming, performing and adjourning."

"That last word doesn't rhyme," Markie pointed out.

"Good catch. Plus, it's negative, so we'll skip that step." Another important quality of a politician—cutting the deadwood. Look how trim and sleek this campaign was. Man, we were humming. I bet people on the street were stopping and cocking their heads trying to figure out where the buzz of success was coming from.

"In a nutshell, today's meeting is all about team building." I pulled out the notes I'd written up during my study period in the library, where I'd researched what it took to develop a healthy group dynamic. "(A) Forming: The group looks to the group leader, me, for guidance and direction. (B) Storming: The organization of the task function dimension—that's when I tell you what to do. (C) Norming is when, um, interpersonal relations are characterized by cohesion, and, uh, I don't really get that one. Pull together, maybe? And finally, (D) performing, obviously, is the moment when people work independently and yet interdependently, which means you do what I tell you in small groups. Group identity, morale and loyalty are rocking on all cylinders at this point."

I looked up from my notes and gazed into the middle distance as if I was seeing a future that the four of us, four and a half if you counted Markie, would forge from the nothingness of our current student government. I closed my eyes, took a deep breath and said:

"I'm working, *we're* working, on behalf of our entire school, for the betterment of generations as yet unborn and for those bratty and ungrateful sixth and seventh graders coming up behind us."

I paused, slowly exhaled, opened my eyes and prepared to receive their admiration.

JonPaul's head was thrown back on the couch; he snored softly and was drooling a little. Sam was looking at pictures of her hamster on her phone and wiping away tears. Connie was having an online video chat with—I snuck a peek—Katie, who was standing in front of a whiteboard pointing to various chemical equations.

Markie was watching me intently. I was gratified by his attention. Then he said, "Look, Dutchdeefuddy: I'm a giant and this is the village and I'm going to destroy it." He swept his arm through the blocks and knocked down the structures he'd just built.

Thanks, Markie, good reminder: if you want anything done, you have to do it yourself.

I love these guys, I really do, but they don't have what it takes to run with the big dogs and I'm going to have to let them go. I'd be lying if I said I wasn't tingling with excitement at the thought of my first staff purging. Everyone does it. They probably teach it in Poli-Sci 101.

Or they should.

6

The True Politician Keeps His Friends Close and His Enemies Closer

JonPaul, Sam and Connie all agreed that they weren't cut out to be political advisors. No hard feelings. They wished me the best of luck and, except for Sam, who goes to another school, promised me their votes.

See? This is what today's politicians are lacking: swift and decisive action, no looking back. You've got to clean house, kick booty and shake your groove thang. The whole political world was making so much sense to me, I was the tiniest bit freaked out. Like maybe I was tapping into a former life or something? Yeah, I could see myself as a Roman emperor. Too bad we didn't have those leafy crowns and chariot races at our school.

Markie, Auntie Buzz and I walked home together after the meeting. Buzz lives in the apartment over our garage, and Markie, of course, was my new roommate. We reminded Goober that he had to get to work when he started walking with us. He'd have followed Buzz home like a puppy.

"I have an announcement," I bellowed as soon as Markie, Buzz and I opened the kitchen door. My family was standing around the counter, eating delivery pizza straight from the boxes. Man, if a reporter from the school paper came over to do some kind of "day in the life" piece on me, I was going to insist that my family have a proper meal in the dining room for the photos. Like the Kennedys. Maybe even some touch football in the backyard afterward.

"What is it, maggot?" Sarah, my sixteen-year-old sister, snarled.

"Hey, wanna hear the longest burp ever?" Daniel, my fifteen-year-old brother, chugged a glass of soda and, um, held forth.

Buzz was checking her phone for messages, but, to be fair, she already knew the great news. It's hard to hear even amazing things a second time and stay excited.

Mom was looking through a stack of mail, and Dad was tying a dish towel around Markie's neck so he wouldn't drip pizza sauce on his shirt.

I didn't imagine JFK had to put up with that kind of disrespect from Eunice and Teddy when he was running for office. I bet Mr. and Mrs. Kennedy made sure his sisters and brothers were supportive. I read that Mr. Kennedy paid for votes for JFK, which, although blatantly illegal and wrong on so many levels, was an impressive act of fatherly support. He probably got invited to the White House every weekend. My family, on the other hand, wouldn't be making plans that included staying at 1600 Pennsylvania Avenue unless their attitudes changed. A whole lot.

But I was getting ahead of myself. First middle school. Then the free world.

"I'm running for student-body president." I looked down at the floor modestly. People like a humble candidate.

Nothing.

Well, another lengthy burp from Daniel and a tiny belch from Markie.

Mom looked up and said, "Good job, son. That'll look amazing on a college application." My mother dreads the day she has three children in college and is forever encouraging us to do things that'll help secure scholarships and grants.

"Go get 'em," Buzz said. "I gotta go. Thanks for supper." She grabbed another slice and went up to her apartment. Buzz's attention span lasts exactly as long as a meal.

Sarah snorted at me and rolled her eyes. I can always count on my sister to react to anything I say with mocking disdain. I looked up *mocking disdain* in the thesaurus to make sure I got the right words to perfectly capture Sarah's treatment of me. Nailed it.

She scoffed, "You? Was there a fatal accident in the chem labs and all the other students melted in a puddle of goo?"

"Yes, it was yellow and gelatinous and now we can't use the second floor and the few survivors have superpower abilities but are barren and albino."

Despite her best intentions to find me repellent, Sarah laughed. And then I laughed when she started coughing because the pizza went down the wrong tube. And then Daniel laughed but made it sound like burps. And then Markie got the giggles so bad he fell off the counter where he'd been sitting eating pizza. And then Mom and Dad got mad at all of us for horsing around and, after checking to see that Markie's pupils were equal and reactive and his skin hadn't broken, went to read in the living room.

Sarah handed Markie an ice pack for his head and Daniel sat him at the table and showed him pictures from a hockey magazine. Sarah and I started wrapping the leftover pizza in tinfoil and dumping the boxes in the recycling bin. We're not the healthiest family in the world, but we are efficient.

"So, seriously, Kev: how are you going to convince the voters to support you? What have you got to offer?" Sarah asked.

I opened my mouth to answer and she tore out of the kitchen. This was mean, even for Sarah. I stood there thinking how sad it was that Sarah would never know the full extent of how suited for government service her baby brother was, when she came back in the kitchen with a tall, skinny, flat cardboard box.

"You are one alien turdboy who should thank his lucky stars that the mother ship dropped off its defective goods with us and we took you in anyway," she said, pulling two posters out of the box. "Because you landed in the home of a genius."

She flipped the first sign around and, on fluorescent-yellow board, in lime-green glitter letters, I read: Spencer for President: The Best Choice for the Best School.

Wow.

The second one was flaglike, sparkly red, white and blue with boingy letters that popped away from the poster on springs: Trust Spencer.

Super 3-D cool.

"There's more where these came from." She gestured to the rest of the posters in the box. "Like twenty-seven. And a map of the most effective locations to hang them in school. Good thing that I went with my last name when I ran for office and that I save everything of value from my past because we can recycle them for you."

"I'd thought maybe you'd sacrificed a unicorn and cast a witchbaby spell and made the posters appear out of thin air." I smirked at her, but even

Sarah could tell I was blown away by the posters. I pretended to remember I'd once known she ran for president. She'd lost.

"What's your platform?" Daniel looked up from the hockey magazine. "What are you campaigning for or against that'll attract attention and make a good impression?"

Didn't see *that* coming. Usually Daniel only speaks in full sentences that contain the words *puck, blood, stitches* or *compound fracture.* He's a hockey monster, lives, breathes and sleeps the game. His skate technical specialist is on speed-dial because having the right boots and blades is essential, and he has a running tab with the guy because he gets his blades sharpened every week or two. Having a weighty thought about something that happens outside the rink is a very rare moment for my brother.

Which made me believe I shouldn't answer him with "I'm only campaigning because I want Tina to be shocked and awed by her great boyfriend."

I said, "I dunno. What kinds of issues do you think are important?" I reached in the kitchen junk drawer for some notepaper. All I could find was a handful of Chinese takeout menus and an orange crayon. Well, I bet the Constitution's rough draft wasn't anything to brag about either.

"You can't go the obvious route," Daniel said, "shorter school days, better cafeteria food, pizza parties every week, shorter cheerleader uniforms. And everyone's sick to death of bake sales and candygrams. You've got to really try to make a difference outside the school. Lead by finding ways to get the students to play a more significant role as citizens. You know, for the community, with the community, in the community."

Daniel was completely on the money with everything he was saying. I never would have guessed. Boring ideas, sure—total snooze fest, if you want my honest opinion—but bound to make me look ah-may-zing in the voters' eyes. "Go on. Like what? I need specifics."

"A canned-food drive for the local food pantry. Everyone can bring a can or two from their kitchens, doesn't cost much and it adds up fast. Very impressive visual. A penny collection is super easy—you put jars in each room and encourage people to dump their spare change. At the end of the year, you make a donation to a worthy cause.

Stuff like that. Come up with ideas, put your own spin on things."

Sounded like a lot of work. Oh well, that's what the student government is for: I'd come up with impressive and meaningful plans. Then I'd make the student representatives implement them. Leadership is all about delegation.

"Those are pretty good ideas, Daniel," Sarah said. "I wish I'd had you advising me when I ran."

"Next time," Daniel said with a smile.

Before I could ask about the interesting things, like power and influence, we were interrupted.

"I like the way you three work as a team," Dad said from the doorway. He and Mom had been listening in. Mom had a neutral look on her face, but her eyes were bright like she might burst into tears and sob about her babies if she didn't keep a tight rein on herself.

I could tell from Dad's big dopey grin that he was a nanosecond away from calling for a group hug.

For a preschooler, Markie can really read the emotional temperature of a room, and he's not afraid of the dramatic gesture. So he gave a little *urp* and then barfed. Pizza doesn't agree with him.

It's not the first time he's yakked pepperoni on my watch.

It was gross, but not as gross as the Spencer Family Bonding Moment we almost endured.

Moving on.

7

The True Politician Relishes the Opportunity to Switch Things Up

I arrived at school super early Tuesday morning, in much the same mood Napoleon must have been in after the whole Elba misunderstanding. Oh, wait, that didn't end well for General Bonaparte. Scratch that, I only identify with the winners.

So—I was feeling fine. Very powerful. On point. On the precipice of turning this school around by doing great and masterful things. I heard trumpets in my head. The blare from brass instruments *should* accompany great statements: *Ta-da!*

I was armed with the posters Sarah had given me and the map of the best places in school to hang them, ready to blanket the walls with reasons to vote for me.

Except that I wasn't the first candidate to have that idea. Or the first one to arrive with a tape gun.

When I walked into the school, I saw 8½" x 11" pages—dozens of them, hundreds of them, thousands of them—lined up at eye level, running along the wall from the front door, around the corner and down the hall. Someone had plastered the halls with an endless line of CA$H 4 PRE$IDENT posters.

They weren't posters so much as pictures of Cash. His image was everywhere.

I confess: he is probably the most attractive human being I've ever seen in real life. If I'm being honest, I have to acknowledge that he's probably wasting his time in middle school. Surely there's some tween-oriented television show with a laugh track just dying to have him be the character that the plucky-and-doesn't-know-how-pretty-she-really-is girl crushes on.

I stopped counting Cash's signs at 386. They were everywhere, an unbroken line of pictures proving that Cash had won the genetic lottery and was a perfect physical specimen. He must have been at school all night long hanging them. Or maybe someone who looks like that commands an army of fairies and sprites and other assorted tiny flying helpers who do his bidding.

Probably just Katie. That girl has an amazing work ethic, so an all-nighter hanging posters wouldn't faze her; plus, I'd seen how she'd melted when she ogled him yesterday. Yeah, this had Katie Knowles written all over it.

The photos weren't even the same image; there were a number of different looks. There was the double finger-point pose I'd seen him do the day before; a moody black-and-white shot of him with his chin down, looking up in what can only be described as a smoldering gaze; him at a beach—his eyes the exact shade of the ocean behind him; a view from the rear where he's looking over his shoulder at the camera and laughing, as if he stood around shirtless all day and, oops, who knew the photographer was right there?; and, my personal choice as the most manipulative and calculated image, one of him holding a puppy, both of them looking soulful and plaintive.

I looked down at my suddenly measly twenty-nine Sarah-created posters and knew I'd have to find another tack. Cash had claimed this form of media for his very own. Anything I did along those lines would make me look like a copycat. And maybe I wasn't as handsome as Cash.

I stashed the posters in the lost-and-found and sat on the floor to think.

All my great ideas and personal charisma were no longer assuring me of victory. Let's face it: we live in a superficial society that values style over substance. I had an uphill battle ahead of me if Cash was going to keep standing around looking that good.

I hated to resort to taking the low road, but I couldn't win unless Cash lost. And by that, I mean I was going to have to make sure Cash lost. I might have to play dirty. I didn't want to, but he was making his campaign all about his looks, and I would have to make sure his reputation was as questionable as his face and muscles were godlike.

Instead of merely garnering support for myself, I was going to have to organize dislike for Cash. Way easier, really, because he's just *got* to be inherently unlikable. No one that pretty can be good on the inside. Except Tina.

Okay, here's the thing: I can't *lie* about him, I don't lie. Not anymore. And I can't really tell the truth about him either. Because I don't know any-thing about him. Except that he resembles James Bond and I'm terrified Tina's going to look at him, look at me and realize that her destiny lies with someone of his caliber, not mine.

So, this change in approach made things trickier for me, but not impossible. Think think think.

Cash is probably the best-looking guy in school, that's a given. But I am definitely the most articu-late guy in school. Double duh.

Plus, I'm *in* school. I'll take a page from the faculty and do what teachers do every day to make us look bad: I'll make sure to ask questions *Ca$h* can't answer. He can't even spell; how's he going to form thoughtful responses? That way, I won't have to jettison Sarah and Daniel's good-for-the-school, good-for-the-community, do-gooder stuff after all. I just have to ask questions Cash can't possibly re-spond to intelligently. How terribly politician of me.

Mom dragged me to a town hall meeting last year during the mayoral election and I couldn't understand a word they were saying. Neither could Mom, and considering she works in a bookstore and reads like most people breathe, that's really saying something. *Obfuscate*, she told me on the ride home, means "to confuse, stupefy, darken or obscure." I'm all over that. Cash won't know what hit him.

The bell rang and I jumped up and joined the surging tide of middle school students heading toward homeroom.

And, as luck would have it, found myself shoulder to shoulder—or rather, shoulder to upper rib cage, as Cash is Very Tall—with my opponent. Good timing is everything in life—and politics.

"So, Cash, I didn't get the chance to wish you luck in the race yesterday. Everything kind of happened really fast. A candidate is only as good as his opponent, right?"

"That's what Katie says." He smiled and even I was kind of dazed by his grin.

Until the words sank in. Katie. I'd forgotten about her influence. Cash was her pretty puppet. I wouldn't get the chance to make him sound goofy, because she'd have fed him his lines ahead of time, given him talking points to circle back to. I know how Katie thinks.

At that instant, Katie fell into step with us. She linked her arm through Cash's and grimaced at me in her attempt at a smile. She'd probably put a tracking chip in his neck like the vet did to our cat, Teddy, so we wouldn't lose him. Katie's going to want to keep tabs on her candidate.

"Kevin." Katie never really says "hi" or "how are you doing" or "did you catch the game last night?" She just says your name in a cold, clipped way that makes you want to change it even when she's trying to be friendly and throws her version of a smile into the greeting. "I never got the chance to congratulate you yesterday."

"I was just saying that exact thing to Cash," I said, fake-smiling back at her, because, for some reason, Katie and I had silently agreed we didn't want him to know we didn't get along. "But I was pretty sure I knew you wished nothing but the best for me." The best failure.

"What a great choice the voters of this school are facing—Kevin Spencer or Cash Devine." If insincerity were toxic, Katie's voice would have melted the paint on the walls.

"I was just thinking how lucky the school is," I said, nodding, picturing myself making my acceptance speech in front of an adoring and fortunate crowd.

We had to stop walking at that point because three girls from my math class came up and asked

67

Cash if they could get a picture with him. Katie and I stepped out of the frame.

"Okay, look"—the real Katie was back, slitted eyes and no-nonsense voice—"I've set up a debate on Friday during lunch for the two of you. We're setting up a mike in the cafeteria and you two can debate while everyone eats tuna noodle casserole. The vote is during last period Friday and the ballots will be counted over the weekend—Mr. Crosby's taking the ballot boxes home with him. The winner will be announced Monday morning."

I didn't want to let her know I was impressed with her knowledge or mad at myself for not coming up with the debate idea first. I nodded. "That give you enough time to bring Cash up to speed with the topics you think are important and have him memorize what you want him to say?"

"It'll be tight—but no, wait! I don't—I'm just helping." She blushed. Pretty soon Katie and I will probably do away with talking altogether, because we think along the same lines and seem to be *thisclose* to breaking the seal on telepathic communication with each other.

"Got ya. So, um . . ." I racked my brain for suitable

debate questions to ask. "Who's, uh, moderating and what's the, whaddayacallit, format?"

"I've already spoken to Mr. Crosby." She looked at me like the fact that I hadn't should be reason enough to call for a public flogging. "Given our—your—time limitations, it'll be a three-question debate. He'll provide each of us—you—with the same question today so that we—you—have time to prepare. He'll ask his second and third questions extemporaneously. That is—"

I cut her off by raising my hand. "I know what *extemporaneous* means." I've had Crosby long enough to know that's how he rolls: he asks the next question based on the prior answer. He says that keeps things fresh, keeps the students on their toes. I think it keeps antiperspirant companies in business.

Good things come in threes. First Cash, then Katie, had appeared out of thin air at the perfect moment. Now Mr. Crosby walked past. Without breaking stride, he handed each of us an index card.

How do you plan to be of maximum service to your school, keeping in mind that, as a leader, you will be encouraging your classmates, teachers and parents to follow your example?

Ah. I can still make Cash look bad, but in a totally acceptable and brutally public fashion.

Like any good politician.

Katie might be able to prep Cash, but only for the first question. She wouldn't have any way of coaching his responses to the second and third questions. And, from what I'd seen in my three-second conversation with Cash and while watching him interact with the voters now (lots of smiles and photos, no chat), he was all sizzle, no steak. Whereas I think on my feet.

I looked up from the index card Mr. Crosby had handed me, smiling. Katie was chewing her bottom lip, and her forehead had gone shar-pei-like. She was studying Cash, who was surrounded by girls. She caught me watching her and tossed her head. Katie's not really a whip-your-hair kind of person, so I could tell she was worried.

I opened my mouth to tell her, hey, since we both have the same question, it won't hurt anything to run through how we're going to answer. We won't be giving up the edge, we'll be assuring a lively debate.

I meant to say that, really, I did. But then I saw Tina—or rather, I caught a whiff of her first,

70

since she smells like cookies in the oven and lilacs on a spring day and new puppies—and I closed my mouth and backed away.

Carefully. Because I have a habit of running into objects or mowing people over when Tina is anywhere near me.

I couldn't risk doing anything that might make me look bad in this all-important, post–first date, pre–second date period of my relationship with Tina.

8

The True Politician Finesses the Fine Line Between Personal and Professional Obligations

"**D**utchdeefuddy."

I was dreaming about Tina. She and I were arm in arm on the stage of the school auditorium, waving to the clapping audience. Cash was sitting in a corner, weeping. His face was splotchy, he looked pale and out of shape and a river of snot flowed from his nose.

"Dutchdeefuddy. Wake up."

Tina smiled up at me while everyone chanted: "KEV KEV KEV." And then Cash poked me in the eye with something soft and fuzzy.

"Hey, it's morning."

I opened the eye Markie hadn't poked with

his teddy bear and looked up into his face. He was straddling my chest.

"Umph." I yawned and stretched. "What time is it?"

"The little hand is on the number that comes after six and the big hand is three little lines past the five. It's four o'clock. Time for breakfast."

I closed my eyes again, trying to picture the position of the clock hands and wishing I had a digital alarm clock. And that Markie could count past six.

7:28. My eyes flew open and I jumped out of bed, sending Markie tumbling to the floor with a soft whump. Lucky I had blown up an air mattress for him next to my bed; it broke his fall.

Oh no. I'd overslept. How had that happened? I never oversleep. It's unheard of. Timeliness is crucial to the success of any politician. Everything appeared to be conspiring against me. It was like the universe suddenly didn't want me to be the political success I knew I could be. I didn't get it.

"The clock started to make a loud noise that scared me but I pushed the button very fast so it didn't wake you up," Markie told me. "You're welcome."

"Why didn't my mom and dad wake me up?

Or even Daniel and Sarah if they saw I wasn't up yet?" I was hopping around my room with my pajamas half on while I grabbed a shirt from the nearest pile of clothes on the floor and gave it a quick sniff. Clean enough. I pulled my Buket o' Puke 'n Snot (best band ever) T-shirt over my head and slid into a pair of jeans.

"They're gone."

"Gone where?"

"Dunno. Everyone drank lots of coffee standing up. Then your mom got a phone call and said a word that should get her mouth washed out with soap and wrote something on the fridge and ran out. Still in her bathrobe. Everyone else left."

Weird. Even for Mom. "How do you know?"

"I hid in the front closet and watched like we did that one time. Your family's not very friendly in the morning." He thought for a minute, watching me try to find matching socks. "Are they zombies, Dutchdeefuddy?"

No one looks at socks, I finally decided, pulling on a couple of semi-clean gym socks and shoving my feet in tennis shoes. "Maybe Sarah. But probably not the rest. Ask them yourself later. Everyone left? What am I supposed to do with you? It's Wednesday. I have school. I have an election to win and a girl to get." As I jogged to the kitchen, Markie trotting behind me, I speed-dialed Mom—my call went straight to her mailbox. I tried Dad—he didn't pick up and neither did his voice mail.

I had to be at school in less than thirty minutes. *Where were they?* They did *not* forget about Markie. Aha! Notes. I spotted notes on the fridge. I bet they were all grateful that I'd gotten the magnetized notepad and held the webinar about the importance of keeping in touch. They'd grumbled, but now our family communication skills were stellar. Reminder: work *that* into a campaign speech.

I scanned the notes, hoping to read that Mom had just run out for milk before making Markie and me a special midcampaign breakfast of chocolate chip French toast with sliced bananas.

H_2O main broke @ store.

Mom

Took Daniel to hockey tourney in St. Charles.

Dad

Kev—you owe me for unloading the dishwasher last night. Your campaign doesn't impress me enough to cover for you.

Sarah

Wish me luck!
Daniel the Puckmaster Spencer

Am I the only one in this house who is trust-worthy and steadfast? Apparently so.

It didn't escape my notice that Mom had just spent Monday and Tuesday with Markie and had probably celebrated something as relatively low-key and calming as unrestrained water coursing through her bookstore. Dad could have taken Markie to the tourney and let him run with the other rink rats. But Dad says his best days with small children are behind him.

I studied Markie and eyed the phone; I have near-perfect attendance, so I could lie and have a sick day. But I couldn't afford even the whiff of a scandal.

I slipped two waffles in the toaster and threw together two lunches. If Markie was going to school with me, I had to make sure he was well fed. The only thing worse than a four-year-old at middle school is a cranky four-year-old at middle school.

I glanced up from slicing apples and saw him stuffing Sarah's old Barbies and Daniel's G.I. Joe figures in his panda backpack. Good thinking, Markie, prepare yourself for the day ahead.

But how to slip a four-year-old under the radar? Hmmm . . . My gaze fell on the flour canister and I got a brainstorm.

I texted Milania: "Meet me @ the flagpole B4 1st bell. Important."

I frisbeed Markie a toasted waffle and he sat in the middle of the table eating while I ran through a list of the day's objectives. The most successful and inspiring politicians always have a plan.

I grabbed Dad's trench coat on our way out. Markie sang and hopped on one foot all the way to school. I made an alphabetized list of adjectives describing me: *astute, bold, cogent, dedicated, effective.* Or would *efficient* be more powerful?

I spotted Milania when we got to school. Markie and I jogged up.

"Hey, remember how I'm running for president because you asked me to?"

"Yeah." She looked down at Markie and frowned. Bummer; not a fan of little kids. Well, tough, we all have to sacrifice for the greater good. Milania could Markie-sit for a little while.

"I need a favor in return."

"You're not even elected yet."

"Details. It's flour-baby week in home ec, right?"

"Oh, yeah." She dropped her backpack to the ground and a cloud of flour poufed out. She bent down, unzipped her bag and yanked out a ratty-looking sack. Some flour spilled out of one of the many rips and tears.

"That baby has seen better days. What would you say if I told you I had the best flour baby ever and an idea guaranteed to get you an A in home ec?"

"I'd say, I'm in. Let's hear it."

"Dump the flour, take Markie."

"Markie's the one peeing in the bushes?"

"Yeah." I pulled a bottle of hand sanitizer out of my bag, compliments of JonPaul, and tossed it at Markie, who dutifully used it. And then pulled up his cargo pants. "He won't do that again," I assured her before turning to Markie. "Don't do that again."

He shrugged, unwilling to commit.

"Here's the thing: I'm in a child-care jam. I can

take him at lunch and my free period and probably even during social studies because I'll explain to Mr. Crosby—somehow—that this is good for the campaign. Markie won't be a problem in art because Mrs. Steck gets so excited at all the creativity in the room that she probably won't notice Markie if I put a smock on him. And we have a sub in science, which means we'll just do worksheets, so I can hide him behind one of the tall workstations. But I need help the other three periods."

"Yeah, all right, but how—"

"You can hide out in the library. We'll get you a pass from your home ec teacher. Say that you're researching child development and need to observe and take notes and research the behavior he demonstrates. Passes practically write themselves when you explain you're going above and beyond the call of duty. Then you and Markie can hang out in a study room."

"For three class periods?"

"Intermittent periods. Plus, he has toys and snacks and a portable DVD player. You won't even notice him. He practically raises himself. He's a very low-maintenance child."

"Okay." She looked skeptical, but I hustled

her off to home ec to speak to Mrs. Nickerson before she could change her mind. Or Markie could pee again. When he wasn't looking, I took the juice boxes and water bottles out of his panda backpack, just to be on the safe side.

Lucky I'm such a sweet-talker. I got Milania's home ec teacher all excited about Project Markie. I could tell by the gleam in Mrs. Nickerson's eye that she was thinking about assigning toddlers instead of flour babies next year. Great politicians always point out the implied or inferred, or whatever, benefits to all parties in every situation. Because people can't always spot the advantages without some help.

Then I stashed Milania and Markie in the study room furthest from the librarian's desk. Luckily, Markie likes sitting on the floor under a table—he pretends it's a cave—so even if the librarian looked, all she'd see was Milania working.

I am a master at crisis management.

9

The True Politician Deftly Sidesteps Problems That Might Arise from an Overabundance of Truth

After placing Markie in a secure location—which is something that happens to politicians, usually former dictators—I went to language arts.

Even though I was dying for class to be over, I acted the model citizen and perfect student as I waited for the bell to ring. Candidates are always being watched. The scrutiny gets to some, but I was surprisingly okay with the pressure. I even snuck a few peeks around the room, trying to spot the people who were watching me for examples of leadership potential. I didn't see anyone studying me, but I probably didn't look up fast enough to spot them.

Tina tried to catch my eye, but I pretended not

to see her and flipped through my notes. It's cool—and impressive—to be so busy and important that you can't even notice the people around you. I hoped she was appreciating how hard I was working to be the right kind of boyfriend for her. She was totally worth all the thought and effort.

After class, I ran back to the library, slipped on my trench coat, did the Markie handoff with Milania, stuck him beneath the coat, which hung to the ground on me, and shuffled off to social studies. No one in the halls noticed a thing. Markie was perfectly camouflaged.

I unveiled him to Mr. Crosby and explained that Markie was my motivation for change in this school. "It won't be long, um, ten years, before Markie will be walking through these halls. I want to leave a legacy of change and improvement for him."

"I assume his mother is in the office, waiting to take him home afterward."

I didn't answer, because I don't lie. I suddenly got very interested in tying Markie's shoe, and by the time I looked up, Mr. Crosby was taking attendance. When he finished, I asked, "So, can I use the class period to talk about the importance of the campaign?"

Mr. Crosby didn't totally buy my act, but he

nodded, looking like he wasn't sure he was making the right call. Now I could practice my public speaking on the class and officially start the public portion of my campaign.

"Gosh, thanks." I tried to look humble and surprised. "In the interest of fair play, I hope you'll speak to Mrs. Skraw, Cash's social studies teacher, and encourage her to give Cash the same advantage."

"Start your speech before my gag reflex kicks in, Kevin." Mr. Crosby doubted me? He must be a disillusioned and cynical observer of government and history. Or else he just has my number.

Whatever. No homework and I got to talk. Two of my favorite things.

I used Markie as a living, breathing, semi-sticky example. "Markie here is but one member of the future generation for whom, together, we're going to make a better school if"—meaningful pause while I looked down fondly at Markie and he smiled winningly back up at me—"we believe in the future and pull together."

I was going to ruffle his hair, but, nah—too much. The good politician knows when enough is enough.

We got a standing O. Little kids are the greatest

visual aid ever. Markie's even cuter than the puppy on Cash's poster.

Katie didn't think so.

She stormed up to me after class and stalked me and a semi-hidden Markie on our way to art class even though it was obvious I was trying to blow her off.

"Can't talk, Katie, no time. Catch you later." I hurried as fast as it is humanly possible with a four-year-old tucked between your knees.

"You're hiding him, aren't you? His mother isn't in the office, is she? He's not authorized to be here, is he? Did you even ask permission from anyone to bring him to school?"

"Mind. Your. Own. Business." Note: I did *not* lie. I merely failed to respond to her questions. There's a difference. Politicians know that you can get in more trouble for what you do say than what you don't. Therefore, keep your mouth shut. All for the greater good of the citizenry, of course.

Mouth shut, feet moving. Katie following. Still talking.

"Where did you get him? Did you *steal* him?" Katie looked horrified. Yeah, right, because every fourteen-year-old guy wants his own small child.

It's barrels of laughs to look after a preschooler. I'd only been responsible for Markie for a few hours and already I was exhausted.

"No, I didn't steal him. He's mine, fair and square." Possession is nine-tenths of the law. I'd read that somewhere. Candidates have to be current with all law, um, things.

"What are you thinking? He can't possibly be covered by the school's insurance policy, nor the legal responsibility–slash–social construct of *in loco parentis* that schools and parents abide by."

Latin phrases. Super smart-sounding. I'll have to throw them around in the debate. Katie's not the only one who can do a computer search.

Markie's face peeked out from between the flaps of Dad's trench coat. "Am I in trouble, Dutchdeefuddy?"

I glared at Katie. See what you've done? my gaze said. Scared the little boy. Nice job. Now go away.

As I'd suspected, Katie can read my mind. Her cheeks got red and she looked down.

"Are you mad that I'm at the big-boy school?" he asked. She shook her head and gave him a crooked smile. "Why did you make a mean face at her?" He tugged at my coat. "We can't make mean faces at our friends in preschool. Well, we can, but then we don't get stickers on our charts. It's important to get along with our friends. That and not picking our noses."

"Your preschool covers all the basics, Markie, but—" Our chat was interrupted.

"Mr. Spencer. Ms. Knowles. Small child. Just when I was under the impression that I'd seen everything middle school had to offer." It was Ms. Lynch, the assistant principal. "I'd have thought you were more of the bag-of-crickets or box-of-frogs kind of troublemaker, Spencer. A little boy is a nice twist."

"Hi! I'm Markie." He flew out from underneath my coat—I can't really blame him, the oxygen level was probably getting a little low and I was sweating buckets—and stuck out his hand. Markie recently learned how to shake hands in a kiddie etiquette class.

Ms. Lynch looked at Markie's hand like JonPaul looks at sink knobs in public restrooms: no way am I touching *that*.

I am oh-for-three today when it comes to Markie charming females. First Milania, then Katie and now Ms. Lynch. What happened to the nurturing maternal instincts in this school?

Why am I the only one who can see what a great little guy Markie is? Obviously, it's because I'm so in touch with feminist issues. Most men aren't really empathetic about stuff like that. Another point in my favor.

"What is it doing here?" Lynch asked.

I hope I never again see the look that was on Markie's face when she called him an "it." He took a step back and grabbed my hand.

Before I could move, Katie stepped over and took Markie's other hand. He smiled at her and I could feel him relax.

"Kevin and I," Katie told Lynch, "on behalf of Cash, after some brainstorming about the deeper meaning of a middle school election, brought Mikey—"

"Markie," I corrected.

"Right, Markie, to school as, um—"

I jumped in: "—a reminder to the voters about what's really at stake—the future students. Katie and I agreed that—"

Katie cut me off, but we were clicking, finishing

each other's thoughts. "—the kids in this building don't have an appreciation of the bigger picture. It's not just about them this year—"

"—it's about all the classes that'll follow us through these halls."

"And you're wrong and mean to have called a child an 'it,'" Katie said in that cold tone that I usually despise but loved her for right now.

Lynch looked like she was going to cut Katie down to size, maybe whip out a detention form, but before she could open her mouth, Katie said, "It would be a real shame, given your hopes for promotion—I heard you have a shot at being named head principal at the new middle school next year—if a complaint were lodged against you for, you know, bullying."

Blackmail! Beautiful. Now we're not just some middle school game, but a real political beast. I beamed at Katie.

Lynch said, "As long as I don't see that *little boy* in this school again, we have no problem. Am I right?"

"You're right," Katie and I said together. Lynch turned on her heel and left.

Katie and I looked at each other and shared another of those silent moments in which we both acknowledged the awe of our stellar minds and devious natures. Markie had to bring us down to Earth. Sometimes he's too smart.

"I thought you don't lie, Dutchdeefuddy. That's what you said." His forehead was scrunchy; he was thinking hard about what he'd heard.

"I didn't lie."

"You didn't tell the truth."

"That's not the same thing."

"Uh-huh." He was doubtful. "And I thought you said it was wrong to tattle on people, but your friend said she'd tattle on the scary lady."

"That wasn't so much about tattling as about sticking up for us."

"Uh-huh." Still not buying it.

"Look, Markie, politics are—"

"—not always nice," Katie said, and squatted down to be at eye level with Markie. "But only sometimes. We'll try to do better tomorrow, okay?" She lifted her palm and he hauled off and high-fived her.

Then she stood up and looked at me. "Right, Kev?"

"Absolutely."

"And then maybe you can both win the 'lection." Markie smiled up at both of us. "Sharing is good."

Oh, Markie, you're such a nice person. And so not cut out for politics.

"C'mon, let's get to art class." I shoved Markie back underneath my trench coat and mouthed "thank you" to Katie. She gave me a "whadda ya gonna do" shrug.

We're growing on each other.

10

The True Politician Enjoys the Growth Opportunities That Allow Him to Reassess His Position Based on the Needs of the Public

I rolled out of bed Thursday morning, ready to pounce into the day like a tiger. *Rrrrrr.*

Markie was still sleeping. I headed to the kitchen, hoping we had some of that cereal that's advertised as the Breakfast of Champions. I should probably ask Mom to stock up on that from now on.

My folks wore serious looks. They were avoiding my eyes and jiggling their keys. Dad was not only clutching his briefcase but edging toward the door. I've seen surveillance tapes of bank robbers in less of a hurry.

"Kevin," Mom said, "I've got the consequences

91

of the water-main break at the bookstore to deal with and your dad has an important meeting. Neither of us can stay home with Markie today."

I studied her. Mom likes Markie, but only in very small doses. I wondered if the water emergency was as much of an "accident" as she'd have us believe.

I turned to look at Dad. His meetings are always important. In fact, when I was little, I thought there was a hyphenated word *important-meeting*.

"No way am I taking Markie with me to school again," I told them, and we all shuddered together at the thought. They hadn't been pleased with my "irresponsible, sneaky and, frankly, reckless" decision (their words, not mine) the day before, but Mom had apologized for forgetting about him and sticking me with the responsibility and Dad had looked relieved to have escaped Markie duty. "And I can't stay home and take care of him either. Not the day before the election."

What'll we do with him? We looked at each other.

The back door flew open to reveal Auntie Buzz holding an empty coffee cup.

"I ran out of coffee and I'll do anything—*and I mean anything*—for a cup."

"There you go! I'm out of here." Dad slid past Buzz and sprinted toward his car. I bolted for the shower. Politicians must always know when another person is better suited to handle a problem. Mom could take this one.

After my shower, I found I had the kitchen to myself. Buzz and Markie were gone. I read Daniel's and Sarah's notes on the fridge—he had early-morning hockey practice and she was meeting Doug for their anniversary breakfast. Sarah makes him celebrate their anniversary every week. I'm so glad that's not the kind of girlfriend Tina is. I'll be relieved to get this election over with so I can start paying more attention to her.

I poured myself a cup of coffee and sat at the table, tipping the chair back and putting my feet up. Even the greatest of leaders need to take a little me time.

I thought about the day ahead. I had a lot of vote-getting to do with only one day left before the election.

"Kevin." I was so surprised that I fell out of my chair. When I looked up from the puddle of coffee on the floor, I saw Milania leaning against the back door.

I scrambled to my feet as she let herself in. She tossed me a roll of paper towels and I wiped up the coffee.

"I came over to walk to school with you. We need face time."

"We do?"

"We need to make plans."

"What kind?" It wasn't my voice that asked Milania; it was Katie's. I looked up from a handful of soggy paper towels to see Katie standing at the back door.

I squeezed my eyes tight and shook my head, wishing I could trade them for Tina this morning. No such luck: when I opened my eyes, Milania and Katie were sizing each other up across the counter. I glanced at the clock. Too early for something like this, but almost too late to get to school on time.

"We'll talk and walk." I all but shoved them out the back door. Politicians have to multitask.

"So," Katie said to Milania as we hit the sidewalk, "what about these plans you were discussing?"

Normally I'd describe Katie as having the kind of interpersonal communication style the military teaches in interrogation classes, but today—maybe I was distracted trying to air-dry my coffee-drenched shirt—she sounded, I don't know, human.

"Look"—Milania cut to the chase—"I know you're working with Cash on his campaign, but you're going to lose."

"What makes you so sure Kev's going to win?" Katie asked. "No offense," she said to me. I shrugged.

"Why do you think he won't?"

Ah! I've heard about this: answering a question with a question, putting your opponent on the defensive. Brilliant strategy, Milania.

"Nice rebuttal." Katie and I admire quick thinking even when it's someone else's. "You know I'm captain of the debate team, right?"

"Right. And you know I'm captain of the state championship–bound basketball team?"

I was walking between two über-competitive girls, suddenly the last place I wanted to be. I dropped back a few paces and listened; they'd forgotten I was there.

"I've been working all week to win over the debate team, the show choir, the orchestra, the band and the foreign-language clubs," Katie said. "They're all planning to vote for Cash."

"I've got every sports team locked down for Kev."

Huh. Cash and I were almost . . . superfluous. Katie and Milania had the situation well in hand.

"What's your interest in the election?" Katie asked.

"What's yours?"

"I want to make a difference in how the school is run."

Milania nodded. "I want to inspire girls to try out for sports because of our success and the amount of student support we've earned through our hard work and belief in our abilities."

Leave it to Katie and Milania to miss the point of politics. Good thing they're strictly behind-the-scenes people. It's personalities like mine—and, let's face it, even Cash's—that are made for the front line of political battle. He may be making a desperate attempt at popularity and I may be in it for the fame and glory that'll make me look good in Tina's eyes, but that's what politics is all about. These girls haven't paid attention to the media coverage of local and world leaders in, like, forever.

I was glad when we got to school and I could ditch those buzz-kill humanitarians. No one cares about the heavy stuff they were talking about; the public wants promises and sound bites and streamers and confetti. Important stuff.

Before I disappeared into the crowd, I looked back and saw them talking. They looked very serious. That's not the kind of expression that makes the public vote for you. Good thing Cash and I were running and not them.

I was so lost in my thoughts that I bumped into Connie, who'd been waiting for me at my locker. She was grinning ear to ear and biting her knuckles to contain her excitement. I was a little leery about dealing with so many amped-up girls this early in the day.

"Hi, Kev. I felt really bad about how I dropped the ball on Monday because I was panicked about the science test on Tuesday. But on Wednesday, I campaigned for you. Well, JonPaul and I did."

"Oh, wow, Connie, that's . . . Thanks. . . . I don't know what to say. . . ."

I always know what to say. But I was trying to sound gracious. And modest. And surprised, even though a part of me was always confident that JonPaul and Connie had my back. That kind of loyalty is the cornerstone of the successful candidate-voter bond.

"What did you guys do yesterday?" I said.

"JonPaul and I went to every social studies class and polled the students about their concerns and hopes and interests."

True politicians shape public thought, they don't go looking for it.

"We had them fill out questionnaires," Connie told me, "and then we collated the data by age and gender. I stayed up late last night ranking the issues in terms of their importance to the student body and—"

I nodded, pretending to listen and to read the pages on the clipboard she handed me. What I was really thinking was that carrying a clipboard is a good look, gives the impression of being smart and organized.

I glanced up because Connie was still talking and eye contact is essential in proving your trustworthiness as a public figure. Over Connie's left shoulder, I spotted Tina.

Talking with Cash.

What is with this guy?

"Walk with me." I pulled Connie behind me and headed toward Tina. I nodded in Connie's direction and said, "Really? The voice of the people is fascinating. Oh, hi, Cash, didn't see you there." I didn't say anything to Tina but I looked at her and sent the silent message with my eyes: everything I'm doing is for you because you smell good and your hair sparkles. She smiled back. Maybe Katie and I aren't the only ones who can communicate silently.

I realized I'd totally zoned out, staring at Tina, when Connie elbowed me and said, "Isn't that right, Kev?"

I nodded, never taking my eyes off Tina. "Oh yeah, absolutely."

"That's really impressive." Tina smiled at me.

It would almost be worth being struck by lightning right this very instant to have my last sight on Earth be Tina's face.

But, wait, what's impressive? I must have missed something Connie and Cash were discussing. So I did what I always do when I've lost the thread of a conversation; I turned to Cash and said, "Say more about that."

He looked dumbstruck. And a little terrified. I hoped I wasn't going to be as scared when I figured out what we were talking about.

"I was just saying to Cash"—Connie jumped

in—"that candidates who really talk with and listen to their voters are the most effective leaders."

The bell rang and saved me—and Cash—from having to respond. We all headed off to class. I was carrying Connie's clipboard summarizing the concerns and hopes and interests of our school.

I could still smell Tina's shampoo as I walked away, and the scent inspired me to carefully absorb the results Connie and JonPaul had given me. I tried to read them the rest of the day, but kept nodding off. It is really hard to keep your finger on the pulse of the people and stay awake. I was glad when the bell rang and I could finally head home.

"Dutchdeefuddy." Markie was sitting on our front stoop, waiting for me. "Auntie Buzz said I needed to sit quietly on the steps and wait for you to come home from school."

I bet she did. I'm the only one in this family who really gets Markie.

"Wanna go sit in my fort?" He tried to hand me a water bottle from his panda backpack, but I was wise to that scheme and shook my head.

"A fort sounds like the perfect retreat for a guy with my stress load."

We headed to the basement. I immediately

100

shook my head again. Poor Mom—she means well, but she has no clue sometimes. She and Markie had built a fort out of pillows and blankets. I know what she was thinking: less mess and he can't possibly hurt himself because everything is soft and hypoallergenic.

But a real fort would be made of cardboard boxes and pieces of lumber from the garage and the old dog crate Dad bought for a quarter at a garage sale because he can't pass up anything in perfect condition that only costs twenty-five cents, even though we don't have a dog.

At first Markie just watched me build while he colored pictures. I don't hold it against him—my work ethic puts workaholics to shame when I'm really jamming.

"Can I pound the hammer?" Markie said in the most hopeful voice I've ever heard.

"No nails. Mom put her foot down when Daniel and I built a lookout platform on the stairs. She didn't appreciate that it was the best angle for watching television." I pointed from the TV to the stairs. "She was all whacked out about having to shinny over the edge of the platform and drop to the basement floor rather than using the steps. You can see the nail holes in the wall and the rip in the carpet where we wedged the support beam. She still talks about that project."

Markie nodded. We both have fun-free mothers.

"She's okay with nails outside, but"—I rolled my eyes—"why would you want a fort where you couldn't see the television? We're not heathens."

"Heeeee-thuns." Markie liked the sound of that. "We're not heeeee-thuns. Who is, Dutchdeefuddy?"

"Hey, you home?" As if on cue, I heard Goober's voice in the kitchen.

"Down here," I called.

Goober thumped downstairs with a box of cereal tucked under his arm.

"I get the toy at the bottom," Markie squawked when he saw Goober digging in the box.

"Do not." Goober crammed a handful of cereal in his mouth and stuck his fist back in the box, searching for the special prize.

"Do too. I live here now," Markie announced.

"See? I *knew* he was your kid. Got custody, did ya?" Goober was grinning. He handed Markie the cereal and Markie dumped it on the floor, looking for the prize.

Before I could jump in to mediate their

dispute—something I'm sure I'd be good at—JonPaul galloped down the stairs. Followed by Sam and two kids I'd never seen before.

"Ihopeyoudon'tmind," Sam said so fast that I felt like I needed an oxygen tank to catch my breath. At least she wasn't still crying about her dead rodent. "ButBeccaandJaredcametoo. Mycousins. They'restayingwithus. Theirparentsarevolunteering. Forthatprogram. Theonethathelpspeople. Tobuildaffordablehouses. They'reonthehousingsiterightnow."

"Cool. A civic-minded family who builds things. They've come to the right place." I pointed to our fort. "Want some cereal? You don't have to eat what Markie spilled on the floor. We have a fresh box in the kitchen."

"No thanks." Becca and Jared smiled.

Nice kids, maybe eleven and twelve. They took Markie outside to play baseball.

JonPaul glanced over at Goober, who was out cold on the couch, a trail of cereal down his shirt.

"Sam got the better end on the cousin deal." Sam and I nodded. "Don't wake him up."

The three of us tiptoed upstairs to the kitchen to make dinner. We used to have a little baking business together, so cooking is like second nature to us.

JonPaul told us about his new aerobic routine and how it was beneficial to his sleep patterns, I brought them up to speed on the campaign, and Sam chattered so fast no one really knew what her topic was.

We probably should have talked more about what each of us was cooking. Because we wound up individually preparing a pan of lasagna, a wokful of chicken-and-vegetable stir-fry and a build-your-own-taco bar on the counter.

Just when I was thinking we'd be eating leftovers forever, Mom and Dad, Sarah and her boyfriend, Doug, Daniel and a skater he was dating, whose name I couldn't remember unless she was wearing her warm-up jacket, and even Buzz and Jack, the guy she was seeing, descended on the kitchen, ravenous.

Goober woke to the sound of Buzz's voice and flew up from the basement to stand way too close to her and offer to get her too many glasses of ice water. Becca and Jared brought Markie inside, washed the top layer of backyard grime off him and made him a plate.

I looked around while everyone ate and talked. Probably discussing their concerns and hopes and interests, like Connie said voters do. Yup, my own little town hall meeting/potluck supper/brainstorm session. Disparate elements of the population coming together in a melting pot. After a baseball game. In the heartland. It just doesn't get any more American than that. Unless you have apple pie for dessert.

11

The True Politician
Goes Down Swinging

Friday morning I woke up a little panicked because it was debate day.

And election day.

Man, we did *not* think this through: the stress of a debate and the anxiety of an election on the same day.

After I was elected, I was going to instruct the student council to draft a policy covering just this eventuality. That's the problem with, um, everything and everyone: lack of adequate preparation.

Speaking of which: I never had gotten around to buying note cards or researching middle school needs or reading the poll questions Connie and JonPaul had come up with or whatever it was future presidents did in the hours leading up to a debate.

And an election.

But that's good, I pep-talked myself as I brushed my teeth and flashed a big practice smile in the mirror. I'm best when I don't have too much time to think. Oddly enough, for a smart guy, thinking doesn't always work for me.

If I had enough self-confidence, I was sure I'd automatically come up with those talking points and sound bites and other memorable speechy things candidates are known for.

I checked to see that Dad was staying home from work to take care of Markie. I did that by reminding him seven times over breakfast and by hiding his car keys.

"I'm not complaining," Dad said, "because what's not to love about Markie"—who was making motorboat noises in his cup of milk—"but didn't his folks say a *few* days? And hasn't it been, like, *seven hundred*?"

"Feels that way, doesn't it?" Mom asked. "Not that we don't love having you, honey," she said to Markie, who gave a renewed motorboat roar in his milk cup as thanks.

I waved a cheery and, for the last time, non-presidential goodbye and headed to school.

Headed to my date with destiny. Or was it fate? One you meet and one you date. I can never keep track.

Getting Cash to wear the paper bag over his head so no one could see his perfect profile was going to be the trickiest part of the day. Ha ha ha. I crack myself up, I really do.

Humor. I'll have to remember that the voters love a good laugh. I am Mr. Funny, so it shouldn't be hard to amuse them during the debate.

I reminded myself I had no reason to worry. It's not like anyone was really paying attention to elections. The voter turnout would be low. Public apathy, which everyone in the media talks about like it's a bad thing, was probably going to be the watchword of the day.

Oh, how very very wrong I was.

Because there was a bunch of kids—the phrase *teeming throng* would not be out of line here—waiting on the school steps and, when they saw me, they surged forward, shouting questions. Believe me, that experience is a lot more interesting to watch on television than it is to see up close and personal.

"What are you planning for the eighth-grade class trip?"

"Do you have any thoughts about how to combat the image of today's youth as selfish and entitled?"

"How will you work effectively with the student council?"

"Will you appoint a vice president from a lower grade so there's a more seamless transition next year?"

"When will the influence-peddling, favor-selling, crooked racket of elected officials stop?"

That last question had been shouted by an adult reporter who'd apparently shown up at the wrong place. "City hall is half a mile away, sir, the *other* building with the flag out front," I said.

My head started spinning. People weren't bored and apathetic. They were obsessed, kind of angry and expecting solid answers and genuine change.

If the public is this demanding, no wonder politicians are unresponsive and distant.

I broke away and slipped into the nearest restroom for a few seconds of solitude. I was leaning against the sink, my head down, when I heard the door open. I lifted my face to see Katie standing behind me. I did a quick spot check: yup, urinals. I hadn't accidentally wandered into the wrong john. Katie had followed me there deliberately.

"Please tell me you're not going to be as trite and cliché as to attempt to cast aspersions on Cash's character today," Katie said.

"Of course not," I said disgustedly. At least not until after I looked up what *aspersions* meant.

Which reminded me: I've got to start carrying around note cards, a clipboard, a thesaurus and a dictionary once elected. To handle moments just like this. No wonder politicians have big support staffs with them; they carry the supplies, leaving the candidate's hands free for shaking and waving.

"I'm glad to hear that. Because I've been—*Cash* has been—working too hard all week to fall victim to a cheap political tactic like trash talk."

"That was Tuesday's plan, but I'm over it now."

"Relieved to hear that." She threw a look over her shoulder toward the door, on the other side of which were the restless voters. She sighed. "Tough crowd."

"How'd Cash do when he got to school and faced them?"

"He grinned and waved, and then everyone stopped hurling questions at him and tried to shake his hand. He signed a lot of autographs, took a bunch of pictures. Crowd control: A-plus. Message delivery: fail."

"What's it been like working on his campaign?"

She dropped her eyes. "It's been fine."

"Uh-huh. Did you volunteer to work for him because he's cute or because you wanted to get on my nerves?"

"A little of both. Why did you run?"

"I wanted to impress Tina and being student-body president sounded awesome."

"What about now?"

"After hearing all those questions and realizing people really want things to change around here, now I want to see if I have what it takes to really do something good for the school."

111

"Me too."

"What about Cash?"

"I don't want to throw him under the bus, because I think he means well, but Cash spent more time deciding which head shots to use on the flyers than he did studying the position statements I wrote."

"Yeah, well, as long as we're being honest with each other: I'm pretty sure I've got the personality to lead, but I think I might not be the most dedicated guy there ever was. I like coming up with plans, but I've never been so good at, you know, implementing them." I thought she'd smirk at my confession, but she looked thoughtful.

"Crazy as this sounds," she told me, "if we could splice the two of us together, we'd be the perfect candidate. I'm focused, you're personable and glib. We both come up with great ideas, but I've got that stick-to-it quality and you've got energy."

"Cash is lucky to have someone like you behind him."

Katie eyed me. I held my hands out, palms up, in the universal sign that means "I'm not lying, I'm not hustling and I'm not messing with you in any way." She nodded. "Thanks. I guess all we can do is hope for the best today because—"

"—it'll be over soon," we finished together. And then laughed and headed out to face the voters.

12

The True Politician
comes out Swinging

The lunch bell had just rung and the debate was minutes away from starting, but I was back in the boys' restroom, standing in front of the hand dryers. I'd flipped a spout so the air blasted upward. The better to dry the flop-sweat pit stains I'd developed over the morning.

The only good part of the day had been that I'd run into Tina as she was leaving school for a dentist appointment. She'd squeezed my hand and wished me luck. I was dizzy from her touch but glad she was out of the building. I wanted to avoid having her see me blow the debate.

Because, all morning, everyone I'd seen had a

million questions for me—the students in this school wanted to elect someone effective and hard-working. Well, some did. Some just wanted to vote for the cute guy. Either way, things didn't look promising for Kev.

The restroom door slammed open, Cash rushed in and headed to the hand dryer to my right. A second later, four sweaty underarms were on the business end of streams of warm air.

"Voters scare me," Cash said. "Are they petting your hair too?"

"No."

"Oh. Has anyone patted you on the butt?"

"Negative."

"Huh. Hugs? Are you getting a lot of hugs?"

"Nope."

"Why are you so sweaty, then?" He hit the button with his elbow so his dryer started again.

"People keep asking me hard questions. They want to know what I think. And what I'm going to do. And how I can help the school. And how I'll inspire the students to make a difference."

"Running for office is not what I thought it would be."

"You and me both."

We looked at each other glumly, arms over our heads. Then Mr. Crosby poked his head in the doorway and called over the roar of the dryers, "Candidates, you're on."

Cash and I checked each other's armpits and agreed that the other was visibly dry. We nodded, shook hands, took a deep breath at the same time and trudged to the cafeteria.

He entered to a shriek of girl voices. I was greeted by some seventh grader who bellowed: "Kevin, are you going to liaison with the school board about the new boundary proposals so that our student body isn't hacked up randomly?"

Milania body-checked the kid into the wall and flashed me the okay sign, assuring me there would be no more sniper questions. She wrangles votes *and* handles rowdy audience members. Nice. Is this how Secret Service agents start out?

I know Katie was there to support Cash, but I searched for her in the crowd. She looked nervous, chewing her thumbnail and pacing. We caught each other's eyes and exchanged waves; I felt better.

Cash and I joined Mr. Crosby at the end of the

cafeteria where three podiums and mikes had been set up.

"Greetings, students," Crosby said. "Keep eating, we've got a tight schedule. You can have lunch and become better-educated citizens at the same time. I'd like to welcome you to the first-ever school-wide president-of-the-student-body debate, prior to the first-ever special election. You. Are. Making. History."

It's Mr. Crosby's greatest hope that, at some point in our lives, every one of his students will have the chance to Make History. He was a lot more jazzed about the election on Friday than he had been on Monday. Too bad Cash and I couldn't say the same thing.

"All right, gentlemen." Crosby looked at Cash and me. "You've been given the same first question ahead of time. You will each answer and then I will ask you another two questions based on the context and substance of your prior answers."

We nodded. I fought rising nausea. Cash got pale.

"Let's flip a coin; Cash, since you're the new kid in town, you call it." Mr. Crosby balanced a quarter on his thumb, ready to flick it in the air.

"Call what?" Cash's voice cracked, he was so nervous.

"Heads or tails. To see who goes first," Crosby explained.

"Oh, right. The one where you can see his face. That side."

I heard Katie moan. She and Milania were standing next to each other off to the side. Milania patted Katie's shoulder encouragingly as she scowled at Cash.

The coin landed heads up. Crosby turned to Cash and read from the note card in his hand.

"How do you plan to be of maximum service to your school, keeping in mind that, as a leader, you will be encouraging your classmates, teachers and parents to follow your example?"

Cash looked like he'd never heard that question before. Like he'd never heard English before. Katie cleared her throat loudly, trying to get his attention. He stood frozen behind the podium, staring at the mike.

Seconds ticked by. I think time actually stood still. I felt myself start to sweat again. No one was chewing, or even breathing, it seemed, waiting for Cash to speak.

"I'm going to need an answer." Crosby gave Cash a nudge.

Katie gave the fakest fake sneeze in the history of people trying to get someone to notice them. Cash finally looked in her direction. She held up a cue card with the words "COMMUNITY OUT-REACH." He seemed to come back to life. But just barely.

"Oh yeah, um, reaching out. That's what I'll do. To the community. Once I'm president. Because that's, uh, really important?" Cash looked at Katie. She nodded and circled her finger in the air, meaning "keep going."

Cash opened his mouth. Nothing came out. He turned and looked at me. I tipped my head, urging him to continue. "What else?" I whispered without moving my lips. "How will you reach out? Details."

He cleared his throat and stared down at the podium as if the answers might be written in the wood. Then back at Katie, who was scribbling on another cue card.

"You know what I think?" Milania's voice boomed out suddenly and the audience jumped in surprise. "I think Katie should be up there too. Vote for Katie!"

Thanks, Milania, way to back the candidate you struck a deal with. But I didn't necessarily disagree with her.

Neither did Cash. He looked relieved and broke into a smile.

There was a collective "awwww" from the female part of the population. As in "Isn't that the cutest face that's ever been seen in the history of the human head?"

"That's a great idea," Cash told the audience. "Vote for Katie! Because she's really smart. Or me. Because I'm already running. Or Kev. Because—because he's running too." He did a double thumbs-up.

I just stared at him. In all the time they'd worked together, had Katie failed to tell Cash how elections work? Maybe he got confused by the idea of a political party, thought it was a "the more the merrier" kind of thing.

I looked over at Katie, who was shaking her head at Milania and frantically waving another cue card at Cash. He'd stepped from behind the podium and was surrounded by some girls.

Crosby made an attempt to get the debate back on track even though he was visibly rattled by the violation of the political code.

"Ahem." He cleared his throat and shuffled his note cards. "Motion from the floor noted. And declined. Because the ballots have already been printed. The field of candidates stands as is—Cash Devine and Kevin Spencer."

Um, wow, ringing endorsements of my candidacy all over the place.

Crosby wiped the sweat off his forehead and faced me. "Kevin? It's your turn to answer the question."

Everyone turned to look at me. I stuck my hands in my pockets—sweaty palms do not win the voters' confidence—and felt something crumple. I pulled out a piece of paper and smoothed it on the podium.

Markie had drawn a picture of us and our fort and slipped it in my pocket. I know it was us because there was a tall stick figure and a short one and they were holding hands and smiling, standing next to something they'd built. Together. I felt warm all over from Markie's reminder of what we'd accomplished and the satisfaction of constructing something so amazing that was all our own. And I thought of Sam's cousins Becca and Jared, and why they were in town with their folks.

"Helping people build affordable homes," I blurted out.

I looked over at Katie. She nodded: keep going.

"That's my platform if I'm elected president. We'll raise money in each classroom with coin collections. And the proceeds will fund the eighth-grade class trip, which will be to a housing site to help build houses."

"Very nice." Crosby leaned forward on his podium. There was a murmur of interest from the audience. Even Milania looked impressed. I exhaled. Crosby started to ask me the second question but the bell rang and lunch was over.

I received a ton of high fives as everyone left the cafeteria. Mr. Crosby shook my hand. "You surprised me, Kev. You usually do, but this was in a good way."

Milania stomped over. "You didn't say a word about support for the girls' basketball team."

"You suggested everyone vote for Katie."

"Oh, you noticed that?" But she laughed and said, "I'd be stupid if I didn't cover all the bases. No hard feelings, right?"

"Nah. You got caught up in the moment. Understandable." I thought of something: "Hey, did you get your flour-baby grade?"

"You were right: Markie helped me ace the project. I pulled an A. Thanks."

"Markie's very helpful."

She handed me a basketball schedule with the home games underlined. So I wouldn't forget my end of the deal.

The cafeteria was empty. Except for Katie, who was sitting on the floor, her knees drawn up and her forehead resting on her kneecaps.

I slid down the wall next to her. "Well, *that* was interesting."

She raised her face and studied me. "Nice job. By the way, that's a great idea. Almost as good as something I'd have come up with." But I knew she was teasing.

"Thanks. Do you have any guess how things'll turn out?"

"The election is two and a half hours away—" she started.

"—and kids have short attention spans—"

"—so people might forget about voting—"

"—and we'll just be a leaderless school." I finished our sentence.

"A nonviolent anarchy."

We fist-bumped each other in hope.

No such luck. Before we left school that day, Mr. Crosby got on the PA system and congratulated us on the biggest voter turnout ever.

We. Had. Made. History.

Yay.

I guess.

13

The True Politician Studies, Evaluates and Benefits from What Others Would Consider a Setback

I staggered home from school and crawled into bed. Markie's folks had picked him up while I was at school leaving a legacy of election chaos. The house seemed dead and empty without him. I could have used his sage advice. Markie always sets me straight. He's like a minion of truth.

I was determined not to think about the election outcome, so I read until I fell asleep. The next day, I showed up at my weekly Saturday morning lacrosse game and then I worked at Amalgamated Waste Management, where I rinse out Dumpsters, from twelve-thirty to five. Then, from five-thirty to nine-thirty, I was at the storage facility cleaning out deserted lockers.

You'd expect, after all that activity, and stink, I'd be so exhausted I wouldn't be able to think. But you'd be wrong. I was still worried about how it was all going to work out.

So I did what I always do when I don't know what I've done except that I'm sure something about it was wrong and I don't know what to do next: I went to talk with Mom and Dad.

They were in the living room; Mom was reading and Dad was working on some spreadsheets.

"We need to talk."

A wave of dread crossed their faces.

"As you know, I ran for student-body president this week." I don't know why, but I caught Mom giving Dad her "don't say a word" look.

I continued, "Well, here's the truth: I only did it to impress a girl. Not just any girl. The most amazing girl the world has ever known."

Mom gave the smallest of nods. Dad, who'd been watching her closely, mimicked her gesture perfectly.

"I faked my way through the campaign all week, but then I came up with some great ideas at the debate. I'd really like to make them happen."

"Uh-huh." My parents looked like synchronized bobble-head dolls as they nodded encouragingly.

"But Cash more than likely has the popular vote. And I think there's going to be a huge movement to write in votes for Katie, who, if I'm honest, is the most qualified person to be president."

"Go on." Mom and Dad were leaning forward, looking a little tense; this is usually the point in the story where I confess that everyone in my world is super mad at me.

"The thing is, I'd be embarrassed to lose, but I'm a little scared I might win. What if I can't live up to all the expectations? And what about Katie and Cash?"

Dad leaned forward like he wanted to say something. Mom opened her mouth to speak. I cut them off with a raised hand.

"So, anyway, I've been thinking: I'm going to email Mr. Crosby and concede the election before the winner is announced on Monday."

Dad couldn't help himself; he had to ask: "Why?"

"Because Cash is the right guy for the position. And Katie worked harder than anyone all week. Cash will be the president and Katie'll make sure he does a good job. I'm going to make sure my ideas about raising money to help build homes, and throwing our support behind the girls' basketball team, actually happen. This time, I'm not just going to talk, I'm going to do the work and see it through all the way to the end."

Mom and Dad kept looking at me.

"It's all about teamwork," I explained. "Just like Markie said when we were talking about the election."

Mom and Dad looked at each other. He mouthed "Markie?" and she raised her eyebrows and shrugged. They're not like me; they don't know Markie as a source of wisdom and straight talk.

"Good talk, Mom and Dad, thanks. I always feel better after we work things through."

I got up and left the room. As I was walking to the downstairs computer to email Mr. Crosby, I heard Mom say to Dad: "See, Michael, I told you he'd start to figure these things out on his own."

14

The True Politician Knows How to Make a Dignified Exit

Even though I withdrew from the race and Cash was declared the winner on Monday morning, Katie wound up as sole president anyway.

Seems that Milania's mother is a talent scout for a modeling agency and she saw all the photos of Cash and sent them to her bosses in New York and, long story short, Cash is now the face—or, more accurately, the butt—of a line of jeans.

He didn't have time to flex his gluteus maximus *and* be president. Katie was thrilled to step in.

Even though Cash is still the best-looking guy in our school, he didn't get the girl.

I did.

Tina showed up at my house Sunday afternoon. I was sitting at the kitchen table, dipping a banana in a bowl of melted chocolate chips, when she knocked on the back door. Just like I'd wished on Thursday.

I tried to speak when I saw her, but no words came out. She smiled, let herself in and sat next to me. So close I could see the freckle underneath her left eye.

"Katie called and told me about the debate and your idea about raising money for the house-building charity."

"The whole thing is kind of a blur and I meant to talk to you and—"

"I'm sorry I missed it. Of all the days to have my teeth cleaned, right?"

"It was, uh, really something."

"Katie also said you withdrew from the race so you could concentrate on fund-raising and supporting the girls' basketball team."

"Yeah, I'm trying to figure out how that's gonna work."

"I have an idea: we could use my grandma's old canning jars for the coin collecting. Maybe we'd even have time to deliver them to the classrooms before school tomorrow so people can start contributing money right away."

"Oh, wow...."

"If you're not busy this afternoon, we could send out an email blast with the basketball team's schedule. Get everyone excited about the upcoming home games."

"Really?"

"After we eat bananas dipped in chocolate chips and watch a movie." She grabbed a banana from the bunch on the table and started peeling.

Did I mention Tina is the world's most perfect girl?

And it was the world's most perfect second date. Totally worth all the crazy things I did to prove myself to her.

Now that I'd *gotten* Tina and didn't have to worry about how to *keep* her any longer, all that was left was planning the world's most perfect third date. And how hard could *that* be?

Besides, I have the greatest idea....

Gary Paulsen is the distinguished author of many critically acclaimed books for young people, including three Newbery Honor Books: *The Winter Room, Hatchet,* and *Dogsong.* He won the Margaret A. Edwards Award given by the ALA for his lifetime achievement in young adult literature. Among his Random House books are *Road Trip; Crush; Paintings from the Cave; Flat Broke; Liar, Liar; Woods Runner; Masters of Disaster; Lawn Boy; Lawn Boy Returns; Notes from the Dog; Mudshark; The Legend of Bass Reeves; The Amazing Life of Birds; The Time Hackers; Molly McGinty Has a Really Good Day; The Quilt* (a companion to *Alida's Song* and *The Cookcamp*); *How Angel Peterson Got His Name; Guts: The True Stories Behind* Hatchet *and the Brian Books; The Beet Fields; Soldier's Heart; Brian's Return, Brian's Winter,* and *Brian's Hunt* (companions to *Hatchet*); *Father Water, Mother Woods;* and five books about Francis Tucket's adventures in the Old West. Gary Paulsen has also published fiction and nonfiction for adults. His wife, Ruth Wright Paulsen, is an artist who has illustrated several of his books. He divides his time between his home in Alaska, his ranch in New Mexico, and his sailboat on the Pacific Ocean. You can visit him on the Web at GaryPaulsen.com.

Gary Paulsen is available for select readings and lectures. To inquire about a possible appearance, please contact the Random House Speakers Bureau at rhspeakers@randomhouse.com.

other terrific stories about Kevin

Available in hardcover from
Wendy Lamb Books
ISBN 978-0-385-74001-2

Available in paperback
from Yearling
ISBN 978-0-375-86611-1

Available in hardcover from
Wendy Lamb Books
ISBN 978-0-385-74002-9

Available in paperback
from Yearling
ISBN 978-0-375-86612-8

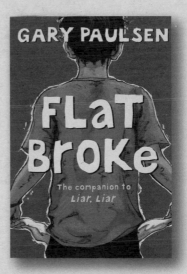

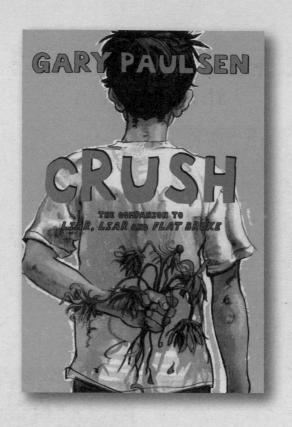

Available in hardcover from
Wendy Lamb Books
ISBN 978-0-385-74230-6

Available in paperback
from Yearling
ISBN 978-0-375-74231-6